ISBN: 979-1-0880598-5-2

Reliquary for a Vampyr

Daniel Robbins

Willowswitch Publishing

CHAPTER 1

"I would never have come to you with this, Abbott, if I didn't think it blessed of God. We are, after all, vowed to do God's work on this Earth."

"Yes, but this is witchcraft. A sin against God at its very core."

"No, Abbott, I disagree. Killing is a sin, but God has blessed war in His name many times. Anything blessed of God should not be sin, for sin is disobedience, not simply a list of forbidden actions."

The Abbott frowned in thought. The brother scribe, taking this as a good sign, continued. "Think and pray upon it, brother Abbott. But consider all that has aligned recently, to make this a possibility. We uncovered the ancient texts, revealing insights into the construction of the heavens, as well as texts for manipulating the heavenly paths between our world and that of the spirit. And Josep de Aramatya arrived yesterday, carrying the holy cup of Christ, on his journey to the old Roman islands in the West. Of all in the world, only we have the ability, training, and fortitude to do this correctly."

At this, the Abbott looked up from his contemplation,

staring the brother scribe in the eye. "I understand all of that, brother. But this task borders the greatest of all sin, the reason Lucifer and his minions were cast out of Heaven: attempting to take God's place and do His work in His stead."

"Again, dear Abbott, I disagree. Only we, the holy men of God that have gathered for no other reason than to study His Word and have committed ourselves to fulfilling His will in this world. If any would be given this task, I humbly put that it would be us. For we would not act out of ego or selfish desire, but to honestly do God's work, helping to rid this world of Satan's influence."

"Yes. I agree. If anyone could do this with the correct intentions and fulfill God's will honestly, with humility and fortitude, it would be we who have dedicated our minds, hearts, and bodies to follow the Lord's guidance, as found in His scriptures.

"I will pray on this tonight. In the morning, if God has shown me His will, it can be discussed with the others at that time."

*   *   *   *   *   *

"It is well, dear Josep, that we return the cup of Christ to you, so that you may continue on your journey. And God speed to you," the Abbott said with an intensity that Joseph, pronounced Josep by the brotherhood of monks, did not understand. And he had thought nothing of it, when the Abbott asked to borrow the cup, explaining he only wanted to examine it and write a few notes about it in his journal. Now, however, the Abbott seemed troubled but refused to admit it, let alone share any explanation. Joseph worried about his new friend and considered delaying his journey west. But the Abbott was insistent, almost as if ashamed of something. So, Josep de Aramatya, as the brothers here called him, continued on his journey from Jerusalem, to the Pendragon king, in the far land once ruled by the Roman Empire.

As soon as their visitor had departed and the gates were shut, the Abbott turned to the trusted brothers around him, ordering them to restrict all access to the catacombs, except that which was absolutely necessary. Now that the ritual was finished, the New Man must reside there until they could verify that he had truly been stripped of all power and memory. As well, they would also have a great task in front of them, to train him in the ways of God, before he would be ready to enter the world.

*   *   *   *   *   *

"Adam is progressing well, Abbott. You should see his progress for yourself."

"Your enthusiasm fades, brother. What troubles you?"

"Well, Abbott, I am certain, that is, we are certain, that there are a few things about the New Man: Adam, as we have come to call him."

My fault if this doesn't work. Bringing a demon into our world. What were we thinking? What was I thinking? the Abbott berated himself. *I thought this to be God's will, but… We may all be damned, me especially. But I just cannot go down there. I cannot yet face what I may have been responsible for bringing into this world.* At the Abbott's gesture, the brother scribe went on, "They are certainly only small, insignificant things. But they are odd, nonetheless. Such as his physique. As you know, he stands taller than most any of us have seen, but although lean as a peasant, his muscles resemble that of any soldier or tradesman. His somewhat larger eye teeth and a disturbing, penetrating gaze have some speculating that he may be looking into their very souls." Thinking he might be losing the Abbott's interest, the brother hurried on. "Although he quickly picks up everything we share with him, including reading, writing, and languages, he refuses to read the Holy Scriptures, or repeat them back when they are read to him."

The Abbott turned to him, startled. "Nothing at all?"

"No, Abbott. We are certain it can only be a willful disobedience. But why he does this, we cannot discern. He will not so much as touch them. Yet he can converse and argue any topic regarding the Holy Scriptures. His only explanation: He states he already knows them."

*   *   *   *   *   *

"Poor fellow, our Adam. He was almost up the last set of stairs, to take in his first view of the morning sun, and he falls into a faint."

"No," the rat catcher said, shaking his head in sadness. "That poor man. How is he now? I do hope he's better."

"Yes. Yes. Mind you, he was looking a bit piqued, even before we tried to bring him up. And afterward, he seemed as if on death's door. But that was weeks ago. Of late, he's been up and around, in the peak of health," the brother said with a smile. Then seriously, he said, "There's something I just don't understand, though."

"What's that?"

"From the beginning, he's pleaded with us night and day, to let him see the sun. The bright, warm, life-giving daylight that all of us may enjoy as we please, but he has been kept from. Then, just as we were bringing him up, he had that feinting spell, and now he's refusing to go up at all. I can't understand it. He'd pestered us night and day about it, but now nothing."

"Hmm… You know what I can't understand?" he said, changing the subject. "The rats."

"The rats? What's to understand about rats"

"Well, you know that I come down here a few days each month, hunting rats, to keep them from over-running the place and ruining all the food and such?" At his friend's nod, the rat man went on, "It seems they've decided to move on, or something. Either that or the Abbott's hired another catcher. I just don't get it."

"I don't think the Abbott would do that. You've always done a fine job for us."

"Thank you for the compliment, brother. But what's happened to all the rats? I used to find them by the dozens and fill at least one good-sized sack with them each time I come." He leaned close and whispered fearfully, "But I've been down here two days, and I haven't even caught a bare hand-full."

"Oh, my, that is odd. Will you be informing the Abbott? He is always interested in anything odd happening here," dropping his voice to a whisper as well, "especially since Adam joined us."

*   *   *   *   *

"…and keep us all under your loving protection, as we seek to find a solution for the problems we face while doing your work. In the name of the Father, the Son, and the Holy Spirit. Amen." The Abbott said, finishing his invocation, in the sputtering light of tallow candles.

As the rest of the brothers murmured their agreement, a sober weight seemed to descend upon the assemblage. Thoughts of service to the All Mighty transitioned to those of the most appalling kind. Silence descended upon them, as they tried to turn away from their repulsion of recent events, and find a solution to the new problem that faced them.

The one they had lovingly referred to as Adam, had revealed himself to be an abomination. Just as they had assumed his innocence to sin from the time he emerged, they had assumed that this ritual of Purification would put things back to right, and they could resume their roles. But a fortnight of Holy torture proved them wrong.

One speaks accusingly – What are we supposed to do, now? You said we were doing God's work!

One points finger – I knew it. I told you so. Using the Grail of Christ in such a ritual…

One defends himself – But he seemed so innocent. A man stripped of his memories, never haunted by his past sins….

One accuses – But he wasn't. Nor was he a man, was he? Drinking the blood of rats! And we may be damned because of it!

One defends the group – Why should we be damned? We were doing God's work!

Another defends himself – Yes. How were we supposed to know? How could anyone know he would…. I mean, the blood….

One states the facts – But he did, and now we need to figure out what to do with him

One questions – Yes. What should we do?

Some plead, a few deny responsibility, at least one justifies their actions before God.

Around it goes, repeating and repeating, the same pattern over and over again.

Then…

The Abbot – We do as we must.

One pleads – And what is that? What do we do?

Others – Yes. What must we do, Abbott?

The Abbot – We must put it to rest.

Again, the circle of debate: first plead, then deny, now agree, plead, deny, agree.

At least one has begun to weep.

The Abbott calls for silence. The room quiets in reverence.

Abbott – Putting aside the method, we must all agree that this must come to an end. We must all agree that we must put right what we began, to undo what we have done. And we must all agree that we must eliminate this abomination. To this we all must agree, though the method not yet determined.

The others begin to agree, first one, then another, a chorus of nodding heads.

The Abbott – From our attempts at purging the evil from the one we called Adam, we know that he is strong, but that he also has certain weaknesses that we do not. Precious metals such as silver, and woods such as rosewood and white oak, cause him pain.

One eagerly chimes in - Spoken words from our Holy Scriptures render him silent, as well, Abbott.

The Abbott – Yes. Where the Word of God is spoken, evil is silent.

Again, the nodding heads, but now a dawning of enthusiasm. The tears have stopped, and hinted-at smiles of hope begin to show.

One wonders aloud – I am curious what Holy Water may do.

One speaks over the other – We will need to use both kinds of wood for his coffin, and bury him at the crossroads.

One who is eager to show his worth – We can bind his body in silver wire. Maybe even engrave the coffin with Holy symbols inlaid with gold.

One not understanding – You think he will resurrect? Is it possible? He cannot be allowed to come back.

One not to be left out – No. Holy ground…the holiest of ground must be used. We will bury him here, where his remains can be protected and watched over.

One who understands – Yes. A demon like him must never be allowed to come back!

The Abbott – Brothers. I have meditated and prayed about this, as I am sure you all have, as well. I have been shown the way. Merely burying him will not suffice. As God's Word tells us, the fires of Hell will consume all evil-doers. So, too, will we let the fires consume this unholy abomination, the very one we set out to save.

One is appalled – Not only will we kill this man, but we will burn him?

Abbott – As we know, we were the ones that brought him forth from the depths. And, as he has proven, he is not a man. It is good that Josep de Aramatya knew nothing of our ritual, and has continued his journey to the Far Isles. We have learned a most dire lesson: that even a demon stripped of his power will always be an abomination, cursed of God.

A few, realizing the horror of burning while still alive, still plead for mercy on Adam's behalf. But, even as the words pass their lips, the truth becomes obvious and inescapable. Purification by fire was indeed extreme and terrible. But it was also the only way.

*　*　*　*　*　*

"But why, Abbott? We've used so much fuel already, almost half of our winter stores. Surely the fire will have made cinders of him."

The Abbott wheeled around, a look of utter dread and terror in his eyes. "Because we must. God help us. No matter how much we burned him, no matter how much fuel we spent, no matter how hot we were able to bring the flames, trying to burn every part of him, his heart lives!"

"What is this deviltry you say, Abbott? How can that be?"

"From the moment we knew this abomination must be eliminated, I knew it to be a task to be done utterly, that no part of him should survive. This is why I ordered the coals to be raked every hour, and all parts set on new pyres built upon the coals. Not only those, but the pieces we took of him during his sanctification by pain: his flesh, teeth, hair, all of it. Even his blood was washed from the floor and put to the fire by our brother scribe.

"If only we could send it back from whence it came," sighed the Abbot.

"But the methods for crossing over from this world to the other, how can we do this? We no longer possess the Holy Relic that powered the rituals."

"We may not be able to send it back. And I would be loath to attempt the rituals again, for any reason. But certain materials may serve our purpose. Materials that symbolize purity, are mentioned as favored by God in the Holy texts."

As the Abbott thought, he also prayed. He prayed desperately, for he knew that time was not likely on his side. After finding the desiccated bodies of the missing rats, hidden in a space dug in Adam's cell, covered by his sleeping pallet, the Abbott felt a foreboding, that time was working against him. And now that the monster's heart still remained, bloodless and still beating, the foreboding had developed into dread. No matter how much time it spent in their fires, it refused to burn all the way. In his wisdom, he knew he had been deceived into this folly. And now the salvation of the known world might be at stake.

"We will do as we once planned. We will call for a carpenter, and smiths for gold and for silver. We will wrap the heart in layers of holy and blessed materials, such as white oak and rosewood, soaked in blessed water from a virgin spring. We will have a box made of silver, with which to encase it, and a larger box made of gold, to hold the secret. Each will be branded and inlaid with holy symbols and scripture. We will keep it here, never allowing it to leave Holy ground. And our order will take a new vow, to keep watch over the blessed reliquary until Christ's return."

CHAPTER 2

Projected onto a screen hanging from the ceiling, a cartoon begins, showing a stereotypical dictator of an unidentified Asian country, with a bad haircut and thick glasses, dressed up like a military general. He's grinning ear to ear, and jumping up and down, waving ecstatically, happy over his newly acquired nuclear capability. It is obvious, from the looks on the faces of the scientists that surround him, that they have very little idea what they are doing.

"For years the world has denied my country proppa support and disrespected us at every turn. Now it our turn, to show the world that we superior," The dictator says, stepping aside to reveal a factory sporting a nuclear symbol. His face showing a child-like glee, while threatening the world with annihilation, as a first step in his obvious plan for world domination.

A narrator speaks then, his voice deep and resonant, "For the last 50 years," the film switches to a shot of a WWII bomber carrying a huge bomb strapped to its underside, almost comically too big for the bomber to carry, "we developed ways to deter upstart empires, from threatening our modern world."

Switch to a shot of the dictator, pointing up into the sky, "I see what you do!" he shouts.

"Some of these methods seem crude," the narrator continued. Switch to a shot of an intercontinental missile traveling across the planet, from one end to the other, "compared to what we have available to us today."

Switch to a shot of the dictator, looking at a radar image. Pointing, he shouts, "I see what you do!"

"And some technologies are on the verge of becoming reality." Switch again to a shot of a drone, flying across lakes and mountains, nuclear markings on its sides.

Switch to a shot of the dictator, looking at through a pair of field glasses. Pointing, he shouts, "I see what you do!"

"But our scientists are hard at work, coming up with ideas that, though not possible today, soon will be." Switch to a fatherly, presidential-type watching an image of the Asian dictator making his threats on TV. Sitting in a comfortable chair, in a dimly lit living room, he turns to talk into the phone, "Pinpoint authorized."

Turning back to the image on his TV, he shakes his head, "Tsk, tsk, tsk. You just had to push it," he scolds with disappointment, as a parent might. "But we see what you do, too."

The camera switches to a long shot of the Earth. "See here, an unobtrusive satellite, quietly orbiting the Earth." The satellite is marked NASA Orbital Research I. The narrator drones on, "Notice the small pod on the side opening up." The camera zooms in a bit, revealing what looks like a gray bowling ball. The sphere is released, dropping into free-fall.

Finally, the camera moves to a shot of the dictator hugging and stroking his comically large nuclear bomb affectionately, his head resting on its side. "Nuclear power," the narrator explains, "The power of the sun itself. Technology not to be taken lightly. And the threat not to be taken lightly either."

The camera then pans out to shot of the Asian dictator and his base. A small, dark object falls directly onto the dictator, and explodes with a very small nuclear explosion, making a crater where the factory and launch facility used to be.

> Next is a shot of a major TV news station, reporting about the unidentified Asian country, and how a tragic accident has occurred at one of the nuclear labs. Our narrator is now revealed, as he reports the incident, "Authorities say the accident was due to mishandling of nuclear materials. Fortunately, emergency relief agencies and hazmat teams have corroborated reports that fallout is minimal and will not adversely affect the surrounding farmland. In related news, unfortunately, no one has heard from that country's dictator, since his broadcast shortly before the accident.
>
> And in other news..."

The screen fades to black and the lights come up in the sound-proofed meeting room. Two Generals and an Admiral clap their hands and, smiling at each other, pat each other on the backs.

"So, this *Project Pinpoint* is what, a floating nuclear platform?" Senator Jenkins asked, killing the mood in the room. "You know what the media will do to us when they find out we're putting nukes in space, not to mention every other country on the planet."

"Really, Blake? You'd think we're going to put nukes in space?" said General Simpson.

"Aren't you? That's what this is, isn't it?"

"Gees, Blake. Just calm down, will you? Okay, yes. Technically, we are putting nuclear devices in orbit. But only technically. These suckers are tiny – a single kilo-ton payload – barely enough to take out a few city blocks. And besides..."

"Wait. One kilo-ton? Why so small?"

"Senator Jenkins, *Project Pinpoint*, is NOT intended as a counter-strike, or any other offensive application, for that matter. Like the film pointed out, it's more of a safety, in case a threat is viable and imminent, but not yet implemented," Admiral Casey answered.

Leaning forward, a smiling man of indeterminate age, wearing a dark gray suit said, "Imagine a bully is about to beat up another kid on the playground. Hit him yourself, you get in trouble. But trip him as he runs by, causing him to break his arm, and the day is saved. No one gets beaten up. No one gets in trouble. It just looks like an accident."

General Simpson broke the silence that followed, "Exactly, Blake. That's exactly what we're doing here. We avert possible danger, and no one has to deny anything, no fingers get pointed, because it looks like an accident. Think about it. The absolute worst danger we face today isn't one of the major world powers launching against anybody. It's one of these little upstart nations, thinking they can wave around their brand new nuclear capability. Or terrorists making threats with dirty bombs. They have us by the short hairs, and they know it!"

"Okay, but what about the UN? Won't they get jealous, or assume we've put up some kind of Sword of Damocles, to hold over their heads? And the media's going to make this into the next Watergate! Mark my words."

The smiling man stood up, catching everyone's attention. No one knew exactly who he was, but everyone recognized the power he represented. "We won't have the UN or media to worry about if only those few of us present know about it. Even the president is on a need-to-know basis. You, Senator Jenkins, were only invited to be a part of this meeting, as you are the functioning chair for project funding in Washington. You're also the most likely candidate for the next run at the Oval Office." Then, to everyone present, "Project Pinpoint has the highest level of secrecy, gentlemen. It simply does not leave this room. Understood?"

"U-Understood. Yes. I'm in. O-Of course. Yes," the Senator stammered, beginning to sweat. He was trying to look sober and convincing, even though his stomach had just dropped. "I-I just wanted to make sure we were covering all the angles, you understand. Just playing devil's advocate, you know? Somebody had to, right?" Senator Jenkins couldn't see anything wrong with the project, as it had been explained. He'd only been trying to turn the attitude of the meeting so that he could leave them knowing they owed him one for this favor. But something about this unknown man in the gray suit scared the politician like no other. "One last question, though. In the film, drone technology was mentioned as being imminent, and I've seen how close we are to seeing a working prototype. But what about the timeline for Pinpoint? How far away from that are we? What's holding it up"?

"Math," Admiral Casey said with a chuckle. He waited for everyone to mentally register his obscure answer, before stating, "We have the satellite technology, the device it will drop, and just about all the targeting data we could ever need. What we don't have is the ability to compute an unguided drop from orbit, into a space small enough to be able to call it accurate – about the size of a house.

"Without the computing power and coordinating algorithms, we could be aiming for Delaware and be lucky to hit Wyoming. At this time, even our largest supercomputers don't have what it takes – not that we would ever drop it on our own soil, of course. But if we can keep advancing our technology at the same rate as we have over the last 20 years, we should have the computing power before the end of this millennium, to make launching algorithms accurate enough to target a single person in a crowded amphitheater."

After the meeting, the man in the dark gray suit walked across the street to the hotdog vendor's cart. "Jenkins will have to be watched," he said to no one in particular, as he waited. A second later, a short man standing a few ahead of him in line, dressed casually in a blue t-shirt and jeans, coughed behind his fist, turned, and walked away.

CHAPTER 3

"Idiots! Pulling their support of my next big project, just because video sales are slipping. Who do they think they are? Distributors are such *duraki* (fools)! I've made them millions in the straight-to-video market these past 20, 30 years: from Blood Soaked Cheerleaders and Bikini Blood Stone, to Vampire Waitresses and Girl School Homicide Detectives." Tuminov shouted over the road noise, into the car phone, as he drove the interstate South West. "Listen. Manny. I'll be in Los Angeles in about a week or so. I've decided to take the scenic route, get my head into the next project, and scout some new locations."

His first box-office hit, Black Streets, wasn't his proudest moment. But Tuminov had a penchant for knowing when he had a good thing, so he'd bought the early 70's Lincoln "pimpmobile" from the studio, and kept it in pristine condition. Since then, whenever he had thinking to do, he'd put the top down, go for a drive in this beast of a car, and sort things out.

With his thinning hair blowing in the wind, he said, "Just like those *proklyatyy* (foolish) producers I used to have to deal with back when I started, Manny. *Oni slishkom mnogo* (they are too much)! What am I supposed to do, take over distribution, like I took over producing? Well, maybe I will."

The nurse at Detroit Memorial Hospital put Dashell Porter on his birth certificate. But he hadn't thought of himself as anything but Alexandre Tuminov, world-famous Russian-born, director of B-movies, since he'd invented the idea.

Dropping out of High School to work as a runner on a low-budget movie set, he worked his way around, taking any job he could get, while learning the craft. Later, he learned a few Russian phrases and began developing his new accent. A unique affectation to get noticed, Tuminov had now been speaking in a Russian accent for close to 40 years. Even now his thoughts came to him with a Russian accent.

*   *   *   *   *   *

Coming out of Memphis, he noticed road signs for the towns of Lehi and Bixby, Arkansas. *More small towns with populations barely more than a few hundred. Hmm. Maybe worth looking at for a location.* Traveling the old highways seemed to calm him, and besides, he needed a unique location for his next big hit – whatever it would be.

A while later, a faded and battered billboard told him to look for "Injun Joe's Fill'em Up Station" ahead. The sign must have been at least 20 years old, as faded as it was. It was fallen and canted into the weeds, but Tuminov could just make out most of a cartoon Indian and a town named "Willow" something before he was past it. Intrigued, he slowed to just under the speed limit.

What he found pleased him even more. The town of Willow Switch introduced itself just past the remains of an old gas station, next to a turn-of-the-century railroad terminal, with a sign on it that read, "Little Joe's Railroad Steak House." The cartoon on the previous billboard showed in the background.

Tuminov slowed as he went through Willow Switch, taking in as much of the feel of this cute little town, as he did the layout and locations. By the time he'd circled back through for the second time, Director Tuminov knew he'd found that something special he'd been looking for. The town had all the old buildings and architecture he wanted. It even had a band-stand in the center of a park, that acted as a hub for the courthouse, sheriff's office, cinema, and hardware store.

Tuminov parked in front of the old rail station, took his legal pad from the glove box, and went inside for a sandwich and some hard planning. *It's perfect! My next big movie will be shot right here. First, I'll map out the locations for each scene right now. Then call Manny to organize the legal team, for all the permits and permissions. Jerry will need to rough out the angles for a script, but that can be done later. Maybe something with a monster theme this time – slashers are going out, after all. Maybe a dark power taking over a small town. Yes! Something different!*

Lost in thought, he came up short inside the door. Pictures, newspaper clippings, and plaques of all sizes covered every visible inch. It was like a history textbook had blown up all over the walls. One article, in particular, caught his eye: a lengthy obituary about someone the town called Florene "Granny Flora" Perkins.

The pictures intrigued him, reminding him of his childhood dream of settling down in the perfect small town, and he began reading the articles and clippings. So entranced learning about Willow Switch's proud history, Tuminov gave his order, ate his sandwich, and paid his bill standing up, making his way around the room. The waitress giggled quietly to the cook from behind the bar, as she described the odd behavior of this short, fat man with the bad toupee. But, by the time he was done, Tuminov wasn't dialing Manny about permits and scripts. "I'm serious, Manny. I've decided to retire. Screw the distributors. Screw the producers. Screw it all, Manny. I'm getting out before I go *sumasshedshiy* – crazy. No, I'm not drunk. I'm dead serious, Manny." He listened for a moment. "Willow Switch, Arkansas." Tapping the picture of a little house on a ranch, part of a recent obituary of a well-loved citizen, "And I've got a new idea I'd like you to help me with. Listen...."

On the other end, Manfred H Goldman knew better than to push too hard. Those closest to Tuminov, understood that what seemed like impulsiveness was really the result of a flexible, quick, and decisive mind, if always a bit selfish in his decisions.

CHAPTER 4

"Originally an order of scholars and scribes, devoted to the collection and reproduction of Holy Texts, the brotherhood sealed its doors from the outside world about the time Joseph of Aramathia made his famous journey, bringing the Holy Grail to King Arthur in the British Isles," the docent's monotone voice reverberated around the room. "The story, of course, embellished from real events, but having lost accuracy in each retelling."

"So many candles in the place, and it's still as cold as a mausoleum!" Marsha complained.

True, the overly ornate sconces, feebly attempting to illuminate frescoes, mosaics, and architectural features don't provide much in the way of heating. But they aren't supposed to, either. William thought to himself.

"And boring, too!" Marsha went on. "Okay. Sure. Like you said, this was a unique, almost British-style cathedral," using air quotes and rolling her eyes, "smack in the middle of an area inundated by those Slavic, onion-topped spires. But, holy crap, man. It's just another friggin' cathedral, Billy."

William wasn't listening, having learned to tune out Marsha's almost constant complaining. *Seems like the only time she'll shut up is when we're having sex.*

"In fact, it is rumored as well, that Joseph of Aramathia must have stopped here to resupply his journey," their guide went on, giving no indication of overhearing Marsha's complaint. "This is, of course, more speculation. But according to experts, it is likely true."

William had to agree with Marsha on one thing: history was boring. The only thing that made it interesting at all to William? Money.

As communism fell in Eastern Europe, museums like the Smithson began sending out experts to scout the most significant collections, once suppressed by the Soviet Union. As these artifacts were cataloged, other experts stepped in, to facilitate their careful removal and shipment all over the world – people like William.

Although he valued historic artifacts, William viewed these artifacts differently than most of his peers, leading to connections with one very interesting gentleman. William had met this gentleman early in his career, and they'd seen eye to eye on just about every topic, especially two: If a rare artifact is going to be on display, does it matter whether it's on display in a large museum or a small private collection? And, of course, money.

And the process turned out very simple. William forwarded a copy of the catalog to be moved, and the gentleman would shop the list around, one or two items would be selected. William would then make sure those items would be diverted in transit. The items would show up at the customer's location, while the shipments' trail was buried in the paperwork, the items never to be discovered missing.

"Moving on. It is here where we come to the next phase in the monastery's history. Having changed its focus and cloistered itself from the rest of the world, the monastery, having survived both World Wars, succumbed to the new plans of the Communist Party. All lands surrounding the cathedral were appropriated and the cathedral itself used as storage for grain and building materials. Once the USSR was dismantled, however, it was opened and portions repaired, to function as the museum you see today."

Between assignments, William traveled on foot, backpacking and using hostels, pretending to be his alter-persona, Billy, to better study human interaction, something William always had difficulty understanding. Although experiencing this odd disconnection from people, he had no travel anxiety, no fear of new places, and actually liked meeting new people. He just did not know why people interacted the way they did. He called himself Billy, when backpacking, and made friends and traveling companions everywhere he went, especially the female kind. Most were temporary...except for Marsha.

Marsha followed him everywhere, no matter the direction or difficulty. At first, he found comfort in their relationship. She made no demands (except for sex), and it seemed comforting not to have to worry about being alone. She was pretty, energetic, and loved to fuck – all the things most guys say they want in a girlfriend. But she was almost painfully stupid, never slowed down, and got off on risky, public sex. What was more, she wasn't interested in art, history, or anything older than 5 minutes. In short, she was wearing him out - both mentally and physically. And she just wouldn't leave!

Why did I think this would be a good idea? William Ferguson asked himself, as Marsha hung onto him, giggling for no good reason. She did that a lot. *I'm supposed to be representing the Smithson Academy to these museums, and here I am acting like any other brainless, college student. Why the hell did I ever hook up with her? I just didn't think it through. And I should have!*

His most immediate mission was here, in the very cathedral he was visiting at the moment – a moment that Marsha chose, to try to pull his attention away again. She did that much too often. And, like now, was always picking the wrong time. The ramifications of his inability to get rid of her was gathering in a knot in the pit of his stomach.

Overhearing the docent talking about an artifact of this museum, dating back to its time as a church, he pulled himself out of Marsha's embrace. *This was the big one! This is the one I came here to see,* he screamed at himself, as the docent concluded, "…consecrated against his return. But of course, that's just the legend. Fortunately for us, the reliquary is on its way to the United States, due to a generous donation by the Smithson Academy, where it will be studied and put on display there."

He hurried to the front, just as the others on the tour moved on. Ignoring Marsha's complaints, Billy stepped closer, openly admiring the subject of the docent's recent comment. The box, about the size of a large footlocker, intricately crafted in gold and jewels, had been meticulously shaped to resemble the original cathedral.

Billy couldn't help but smile, not just at the beauty of the reliquary, but at the amount of money that would serve to enrich his off-shore account.

*   *   *   *   *   *

Months of work! All the patience, time, and effort. Effing Marsha has to go eff it all up! William thought from the back of the Interpol vehicle. *She's got to be the one. She must have blabbed.*

"So, what kind of conviction do you think we can get?" asked the junior officer in broken French.

Crouching together, under the junior officer's umbrella, Interpol Chief Detective Jean De Couvrir replied, "The conviction will be easy. We've been on this one's trail for quite a while and collected enough evidence to put him away a minimum of 80 years."

"That long? So why the sad face, Sir?"

William could see the patrolman talking to the Interpol agent across the street, but couldn't make out anything they were saying, due to the rain running down the squad car's windows. *At least I got that reliquary shipped off. Payment was verified in my Cayman account this morning. What am I facing? 5 years with the right lawyers? Effing trial's going to take half that, just to convict me. Yeah. It won't be easy, but I can do that. Meanwhile, my little nest egg is earning 4.4%. Enough to retire on and live comfortably in Brazil, once this is all over.*

The Interpol detective looked up from the water flowing over the tips of his shoes, studied the fresh-faced officer for a moment, then replied, "It isn't the conviction I am worrying about. Extraditing him out of your country is the greater concern."

The junior officer nodded for him to go on.

"You couldn't be that naïve to your own laws, could you?"

"I'm not naïve, sir. I assure you," drawing himself up in umbrage.

"Relax, will you? I meant no insult. Perhaps your professors skipped over the laws pertaining to the preservation and transport of artifacts, to concentrate on those more pertinent to your daily duties," he said, waving a hand in dismissal. "The Moldavian government has laws dating back to almost the middle ages, dictating punishment for crimes like these. Rather severe laws, that have yet to be revised according to modern standards. It is my fear, that I will not be able to take Mr. Furguson back with me, which means he will be facing a sentence of death."

The young officer's face dropped. "Whew. I had no idea, Sir. I guess I have some studying to do." The junior officer turned, looking across the street, where William waited in the patrol car. "Poor fellow."

William saw the sad look on the junior officer's face, as they made eye contact. *Effing cops. Effing Interpol, too! Just got lucky. That's all. And I'm betting it was something Marsha said. Little slut just can't keep her mouth shut. I'll have to get a message out through my law team. Have someone sent out to teach her a good lesson, shut her up for good!* William relaxed back into the back seat. *Yeah. I just need a good team of lawyers and everything's going to turn out just fine.*

CHAPTER 5

Flora Perkins, the last survivor of the Perkins family legacy, baked some of the best fruit pies in the entire county and acted as if she were related to everyone in town. All three of her boys, however, lost their lives in service to their country. Everyone in town knew, when she passed away, that she'd left the sale of her house and ranch property to Operation Homefront, a non-profit organization dedicated to assisting the families of military personnel and veterans.

Almost 10 years passed, however, before anyone contacted the bank regarding the property's sale. At first, the townsfolk were happy to hear that her final wish was at last fulfilled. Shortly afterward, however, their happy thoughts turned to mild curiosity about just who the buyer could be. Someone from the outside, surely, but who? As time passed, the wheels of gossip rolled through town like a teenager cruising in his dad's new convertible.

— He's a city man, so he must be rich.

— I bet he's super-rich.

— If he is, I bet he's famous.

— He's probably some kind of slick wheeler-dealer.

— What if he's just an investor-type, and we never get to see him?

— Yeah. The ranch is just the first step. Next thing you know, he'll be buying up the town.

— No. I bet he's rich and famous. Gotta be.

— And handsome, like Rock Hudson!

— Rich, famous, good-looking... Maybe he's an actor.

— Yeah! Maybe we've seen his movies.

Then a contractor arrived, with all the modern equipment and workmen necessary to renovate the Perkins' large, but modest, four-bedroom ranch house, and the small flame of casual speculation became a raging bonfire of curiosity. Everyone wanted to know anything they could about this mysterious buyer. When one of the contractors let slip the big boss was indeed from Hollywood, rumors blazed up and down the fences.

Expecting the old Perkins place to have been renovated and upgraded, the citizens of Willow Switch were absolutely appalled to find it leveled and quickly rebuilt into a sprawling, California Mission-style mansion.

Then, expecting a tall, heroic, handsome, and rich owner to take possession, they stood absolutely aghast when they caught sight of Alexandre Tuminov. Although the Hollywood director was super rich, he was also a short, pudgy, balding individual. Not only that, but being used to having his every demand met by assistants for the last 30 years, the townsfolk soon learned he was also quite annoying. Not only did he act the "big-shot," he quickly went from annoying to obnoxious, as he commented openly about everything, seeming not to notice the people around him at all, as if they were just part of the scenery on the set of the movie about his life.

When Tuminov arrived, he did so in a 1972 Lincoln convertible, wearing an expensively tailored, if out of date, suit. He wore a Rolex on one arm, and an aging bimbo on the other - big hair, tight, leopard print dress, garish makeup and all. She even spoke in a whiny, Brooklyn-accented baby's voice, just the way a gangster's moll might have in one of those old movies.

In Hollywood, these annoying details and Tuminov's obnoxious behavior were only out of the ordinary enough to get him noticed, get him results, and get him respect. In Hollywood, his manner and attitude forced meetings, demanded backing, helped him get things done his way, and never allowed him to look back at failure. But among the simple community of farmers of Willow Switch, Arkansas, it only made him a pariah, avoided and derided at every opportunity.

To the world-famous Director Tuminov, it was all like water off a duck's back. He didn't notice and he couldn't care less. He was retiring in the kind of little town he'd always dreamed of settling down in and figured the world still revolved around him.

All of the animosity Alexandre Tuminov earned, did indeed have an effect, however. Mrs. Bonnie Tuminov-Sinclair, born Bertha Mae Landstein, had only ever wanted to fit in. As a girl in the Bronx, she was too heavy-chested to fit in with the other girls and too slow to fit in with adults. In Hollywood, she knew people made nice to her, because of her husband. But even there, she knew she didn't fit in. In fact, the only place she felt like she fit in was with Alex (her little "Toomie"). They'd met when she was a starving actress. Starving because she didn't have much talent, just a body that attracted wolves. And she quickly found out that most casting directors only offered parts if an actress would put out.

Tuminov was different. He only wanted to know if she could scream decently, and that she wouldn't mind taking off her top for the camera whenever the script called for it. Since the only other work she'd been able to find was at a local strip club, under the name "Bunny," Bonnie Sinclair became a B-movie sensation.

In all honesty, Mrs. Tuminov-Sinclair had to admit she'd married her husband out of frustration and loneliness. He was rich and seemed to offer the only way out of a dream-shattered life gone bad. But, like Hollywood, marriage to the world-famous director was not what she'd imagined either. She'd fooled herself into believing she'd finally grabbed the brass ring, but he was dominating and selfish. She was his trophy, not her salvation. To protect herself, she was always loyal anyway. And she worked hard at living the lie. Over time, however, her disappointment was tempered by something few in her position ever find. Bonnie Tuminov-Sinclair found love.

*   *   *   *   *   *

She didn't know why she'd thought of it. Although she thought about her sister a lot, Lt. Drukner hadn't thought about the letter in a long time. It began "We regret to inform you," and ended "with condolences." One of those letters parents never want to receive about their children. *If you're not a parent, you think you'll never get one, right?* She'd gotten this one over a year ago, when she was still working on the millennium upgrade, here at NORAD. Although the letter told her of her sister's death, three more weeks would pass before the next one, telling her the cause of death: heart failure due to exhaustion and malnutrition. *Emily was working so hard at university, that she'd neglected to take care of herself, to such an extreme...*

"You mind if I sit here? Thanks so much. Saw you sitting by yourself, and I thought to myself, *Jenny? You need to go sit with that ol' sad-sack over there right quick."* The newcomer babbled, sitting down even before the request for permission was out of her mouth. Lou wasn't sure who Jenny was, but she spoke quickly and acted impulsively, reminding Lou of one of those fairies in the old cartoons. "Second Lieutenant Jennifer Ludlow," she said, still smiling, extending her hand, "and you are?"

"Sorry. Lieutenant Druckner. Louvenia. Um, Lou," she stammered, taken aback by the abrupt interruption.

"Jenny. Pleased to meet you." She said while looking over Lou's shoulder. "Check out the hot one over there!" Before Lou could react, Jenny had already waived flirtatiously at the man, and shifted her attention back to Lou. "What about this Pinpoint thing we're working on, huh? Secret, secret, am I right? So exciting!

"Yeah, we're not supposed to mention anything about it outside of the lab. Not even the name of the project, right?" Lou chided quietly.

"Oh, yeah. Mum's the word. Sure." After almost an entire minute, "But it's way cool, though, right? I only got the tiniest of briefings on it. Today's my first day. My first assignment is the testing schedule." Jenny didn't have much on her plate, but she wolfed it down quickly, all while somehow talking non-stop. Lou quickly gave up on trying to get a word in edge-wise and just sat back and listened.

Jenny never seemed to stop smiling, as if life were actually fun. And she talked about everything under the sun, skipping from subject to subject, seemingly without rhyme or reason. *For someone that just arrived, how does she know so much?* Jenny talked so fast Lou could barely keep up. One thing that stuck, however, was the mention of Corporal Blake down in the Armory, who made the best cup of coffee. Apparently, he had a source that would get him some of the best beans, that he would roast in his homemade setup. Lou loved coffee, and not just because she was in the armed forces. *There's just something about it,* Louvenia thought, *almost as if it spoke to my soul. Okay. That's a weird way to put it. But I HAVE to make my way down there and try it!*

After Jenny left, Lou's mind went back to thinking about her sister, and how much Emily wanted to be a doctor. She missed her sister but had to admit she was haunted by the decisions she'd made, avoiding her family duty. *Emily always took care of everything. Was it too much to ask her to just keep taking care of stuff? Leaving after high school wasn't such a bad thing. And I needed to get out of there! Look at where I am now. It all worked out okay, right? I mean, she got to go to university and pursue her dream. It isn't my fault she pushed herself that hard. It isn't my fault she died!*

*   *   *   *   *   *

"Chicken! Fried frickin' chicken, Vern!" Lindsey Mae said, storming into the kitchen.

"Fried chicken. Right," with a shrug of his shoulders, "What about it?"

"This is a steak house, Vern. Our menu's one page." Linsey Mae threw up her hands. "We got steaks, we got hamburgers, we got beer. What we ain't got…. Oh, let's see, Vern. Frickin' CHICKEN!"

"And…"

"And," she said dramatically, her eyes popping wide with disbelief. Then placing her hands on her hips for emphasis, "Ain't no fried chicken on the menu, Vern.

"That fat, ugly, Hollywood producer's fancy-ass bimbo out there spent the last 10 minutes makin' me wait to take her order. Makin' me miss tips, while she sat there studyin' the dang menu. Then she finally puts the thing down, looking off into the horizon, and actually says 'I'll have the fried chicken' – as if its actually there on the menu!"

Vern took a second, returning the waitress' stare with a sigh of his own. "What's the big deal? Jus' take \$10 from the till and run down the street."

The prettiest girl in school, Miss Lindsey Mae Atkins wasn't the sharpest knife in the drawer. But she caught on after a minute. "You mean the broaster place?" she said in disbelief.

"Yeah." Vern said, relieved he didn't have to spell it out for her. "Call it in from here and go pick it up. I'll put it on a plate, all fancy-like. Problem solved. Everyone's happy."

"Seriously?" she said. "Really. You really are serious."

"Go! But hurry back, Lindsey Mae, so your orders don't pile up"

Rolling her eyes dramatically and throwing up her hands again, "Fine. I'll call it in, but I'm sendin' Jimmy-Wayne to go get it. I'm not missin' out on tips, just fer some stupid bimbo don't know how to read a frickin' menu."

* * * * * *

In little towns like Willow Switch, there are always little jobs that need doing, jobs that seem too small, too dirty, or too odd to call out a professional: road kill removal, septic tank digging, stump removal, fence replacement, pumping out a flooded basement. The Willis boys were the ones everyone called. The three Willis brothers were willing to go anywhere and do just about anything, at any time of day, as long as it paid cash.

Beau, Austin, and Cody worked hard because they liked making money. Money paid for their "relaxation." And the Willis boys were all about relaxing. Their latest round of relaxation arrived in frosty mugs, placed on the table, with a huff of annoyance, by their favorite waitress, Miss Lindsey Mae Atkins.

Their whoops of laughter and attempts to pinch her butt died in disappointment, as they realized she wasn't playing along. So, they grabbed their beers and started looking around for the next distraction.

Middle child Austin, being the sharpest of the bunch, noticed them first. "Whoo, doggies! Will you look at that there?"

Beau, older than Austin, said, "Wazzat?" Then, seeing who his brother meant, "Oh. Them?"

Youngest brother Cody recognized them, "That's that Hollywood feller, ain't it?"

With the height and breadth of a linebacker, Beau had been destined for athletic stardom from the age of eight. But a bad hit during a High school football game cost him the brain power for all but the simplest directions. From that day, Beau satisfied himself doing most of the trio's heavy work. "Yeah. I 'ermember," he said, brows knit together in heavy thought. "His name is... toon-somthin', right?"

"Yeah, yeah. Toon-somthin.' Ain't that right, Austin? Toon-somethin', right?" Cody parroted.

"Tuminov. Too-min-ov," Austin sounded out.

"Yeah. Toomie-nov," said Beau in his slow manner.

Cody burst out, "Toomie! Ha-ha-hee. Toomie! Ha-ha-hee. That's funny, right, Austin? Toomie." Beau could be slow to understand a new idea, but Cody set the record for simple. But, unlike Beau, Cody couldn't blame an accident.

But Austin wasn't concerned with the little fat man. "Will ya look at the knockers on that gal of his?"

"Whoo-Wee!" Beau said in disbelief.

Like an excited weasel, Cody could hardly keep his seat. "Yeah. Whoo-Wee! Whoo-Wee, alright. Whoo-Wee."

"Like ta git me some o' dat der." Beau slurred.

"Yeah, boy! Some o' dat der! Git me some o' dat! Right, Austin? Some o' dat."

Austin leaned close, looking each of his brothers in the eye, "Shh! Don't want 'em hearin' us. They might get the wrong idea 'bout us easy-goin' type guys."

"Yeah, shush up, Beau. Don't want 'em getting' the wrong idea."

"Huh?" Beau said, "Like what, we wan' 'em ta come over here an' sit with us, er somethin'?"

"Sit with us? Ha-ha-hee! Yeah. The girlie can, anyways."

"Naw!" Austin said sourly. "Don't want 'em thinkin' we ain't neighbor-like. We don' wanna be rude, now do we?"

"No, sir. I ain't rude. Mamma always taught me to be po-lite." Beau said carefully. "Mamma never would like it if'n we were ever rude to folk."

A look of innocence crossed Cody's face. "I ain't rude neither. Am I Austin? Mamma'd never'd liked that. She'da skinned us fer catfish, if'n we were bein' rude!"

Ignoring his brothers' comments, "Besides, boys," Austin said with a sly look, "I'm getting' an idea."

"Yeah?" Beau and Cody said together.

"Yeah..." Austin said with a sly look crossing his features.

After a minute of waiting, Beau and Cody chimed together, "Well?"

Austin spoke low, "See the ways they's dressed? All fancy-like and jewelry and such?"

Understanding that the look on Austin's face meant he was getting one of his slick ideas, "Yeah? Yeah?" said Beau and Cody leaning closer.

"Well, we know they come from Hollywood and all, been in the pichers and such. Moved into that big ol' bran' new house and all. So, we knows they's rich. Well, I'm just wanderin' HOW rich?"

Trying hard to show he understood, Cody said, "Must be rich, I bet. I bet they's real rich. Big ol' house an' all."

"I's just thinkin' how them bein' new to the area, and us bein' neighborly an' all, mebee we should pay 'em a little visit."

"What? You wants they should be friends o' ours?" asked Beau.

"Yeah, yeah," Cody said, looking back and forth at his brothers, like a spectator at a tennis match. "You wants they should be friends o' ours? Why'd we want them's as friends, Austin?"

Austin often reflected that Beau's slow, drawn-out manner was frustrating enough for him to want to punch him, just to make him speak faster. But it was Cody's quick interjections, often just repeating what Beau said, that interrupted Austin's anger, causing the tension to drain away.

"And they's a couple a," Beau searched for the word, "weirdos, too. No tellin' what kind of stuff they got up there in that big ol' house o' theirs."

"That's jest it," Austin said. "Rich folks, all by themselves, in a big ol' house, all furnished with rich folk stuff. An' them bein' all alone, 'cause no one ever goes out ta visit 'em."

"Yeah! No one goes out there, 'cause they's weirdos!" Cody agreed.

"And you want us to make all friendly-like and...," said Beau, working to connect what Austin was saying.

Raising his brows expectantly, "Rich. Alone. No one comin' around to check on 'em…"

Beau's mind continued to work, "Ahh! And we could just be them neighborly, friendly-like folks to come out and visit 'em like that."

Tapping the side of his nose, Austin supplied, "And mebee they'd let us stay a while. Mebee share a bit o' what they's got with us."

"And mebee give us some nice little partin' gifts when it comes time fer us to leave," a smile of understanding crossing his features.

"Now yer getting' it, Beau," Austin said.

"Boy! Do you ever have the best ideas, you do."

Brows furrowed, Cody said, "Idea fer what? I still don' get it."

Austin sighed irritably, "We ACT like we's friends and such, goin' over there all friendly-like, and we gets 'em to let us stay wit' 'em fer a while. Then we grab the best stuff we can, and we skedaddle out o' there a'fore they can do anythin' 'bout it."

"Maybe we can go to Bixby. I like Bixby. I bet we could sell all kinds o' stuff in Bixby."

"Sure, Beau! Maybe stay there a while, livin' high on the hog, a'fore we come back to diggin' septics."

"Yeah, Austin! Like a vacation!" Beau said, clapping his meaty hands together with childish glee.

Cody still didn't understand, but he knew what a vacation was. "I needs a vacation," he said with relief.

"Well, its settled then, boys! We'll go visit our new friends. Then we can take a couple o' weeks off an' go have ourselves a good time. What do you say?"

"I'm in, brother."

"Woo-Wee! Me, too!"

CHAPTER 6

Mr. and Mrs. Tuminov turned into their driveway, one focused on his newest acquisition: a golden reproduction of one of the oldest cathedrals in Romania. The reliquary was not the first of such finds, however. Tuminov had acquired a few paintings and statuary from the same area, all Eastern Orthodox, all ancient, all priceless, and all stolen. *Stolen is such a harsh word,* he corrected himself. *Diverted in transit. I like that better.* Tuminov, having shot films all over the world, had friends in the shipping industry that, for a modest fee, were willing to replace a shipping label or two on a larger shipment of relics from Eastern Europe to the US. *As long as it is coming here anyway, I should be able to have a bit of a private showing, yes? I am not a thief, just a borrower. It will be returned. Of course, it will be returned. Eventually, it will be returned. Just not yet.* He smiled to himself, as he opened the front door, forgetting to hold it for his wife.

Bonnie, however, was in a bit of a funk. She was torn between yelling at her husband and throwing her arms around him, like a child, seeking safety and assurance. She loved her "Little Toomie," but he could be so annoying sometimes. Like just now, opening the door and pushing his way inside, without a thought for her. *He almost locked me out just now! How could he be so thoughtless?! But he's been distracted lately. I should cut him a break. He really loves it here.*

Although moving away from the grind of Hollywood had been a blessing, it had also turned into something of a curse, as well. It was nice not having to play the part of the Happy Hollywood Housewife with the other high-roller's wives. But she felt a bit like the wife in that old TV show, the rich one that had moved out to the country with her husband because he wanted to be a farmer more than he wanted to be a lawyer. She missed the stores and the fine clothes, as well as the parties and the celebrity awards functions. *Well, I don't miss the false fronts and painted smiles,* she thought.

It was different here. But not much better. She still saw false smiles and knew she was talked about behind her back. That it was more obvious, seemed to somehow decrease the pain it inflicted, but not by much. She'd imagined going to the store for groceries like normal people did. But the one time she'd done so, all the whispers behind hands and disapproving looks, caused her to abandon her items in the cart and run out crying. In her heart, she'd known that sort of thing would happen. She'd tried her best to ignore the open stares and pointed fingers. But in the end it was too much for her. And now she loathed to even set foot outside of their house.

While her husband ran to his study, where the new crate had been placed, his attention focused on his newest piece of contraband art, Bonnie stuffed their coats into the closet. *Yeah, Toomie. I know how you got it. I may not be the sharpest tool in the shed, but I'm not THAT stupid.* She sighed. *I just wish you'd pay that much attention to me, once in a while.* She barely noticed she hadn't hung the coats up very well, when the front door beside her banged open, revealing three men wearing grungy overalls.

"Well, Howdy, neighbors!" said the first with a big smile. He was a smaller version of the bigger one just behind him.

"Yeah. Howdy, neighbors! Howdy!" the scrawny one bringing up the rear parroted. "Ha-ha-hee!"

*   *   *   *   *   *

Focus, girl. Just focus. Got to get caught up, before Westbank notices! I'm not too far behind, right? If I can just block out those stupid dreams! I can't stop thinking about them. So weird...

"Lieutenant? Could you come into my office, please?" Major Westbank said from the doorway, breaking into Lou's thoughts.

Oh, crap! He can't have noticed my productivity's down yet. Can he put me on report for that? Luvenia asked herself, petrified of confrontations, especially with her boss. *How did he find out so quickly?*

"Shut the door, Lieutenant. This won't take a minute." Westbank took a folder from his pristine desk. Placing it neatly into the file cabinet, he tried to put on his most serious face as he sat down.

Taking a moment to straighten his posture, he began, "As you know, this project is very important to the brass, and must stay on schedule. To do this, we must all do our parts, and keep from falling behind. Which brings me to the topic of this meeting. The testing schedule has been moved up. I need everyone on top of their game.

"It has come to my attention that your attention might be slipping lately, Lieutenant. Bothered by dreams, I think it was." Westbank paused uncomfortably. *Managing people gently is just not my forte'. I can't just order this woman to get her head back in the game, darn it!*

"Well. So far, this project is on track. But I cannot allow anyone to let it fall behind. I need to know that these dreams, or whatever, that have you so distracted, will be dealt with ASAP." Lou might have seen the humor of his embarrassment, were it not for the seriousness of meeting with her commanding officer. Even the most casual interaction was stressful when dealing with someone that could break your career at the slightest disappointment. And Major Elliot E. Westbank was a ball-breaker.

Lt. Luvenia Drukner stood gaping. *How did he find out so quickly?* She'd only been having these weird dreams the last few days. *Okay, yes, it has been affecting my work a little. But not so bad I can't catch up! Jeez! Westbank notices everything!* Which, she had to admit to herself, was why he was so good at managing projects like this.

"I wish you could see yourself. Your reaction confirms my suspicions." Lou's mind was working in different directions at that moment. *How did Westbank find out? I never told anyone about my dreams bothering me.* Then it came to her in a flash, and she almost hit herself, as she remembered her brief comment to Jenny at morning chow. *Boy! She works fast. Then again, this is Jenny, right?*

"Now listen, Drukner. I'm not entirely without heart. I'd like to help. Really, I would. You don't have to confide in me. I don't need to know the details. I just want to know one thing: Is this something we can do something about, or do I need to start looking for another genius programmer?"

Shutting her mouth and slamming herself into full attention. "Just throwing me a bit off, Sir. Nothing to worry about. It's just a temporary distraction. I'll get myself focused and redouble my efforts, Sir. You have my promise."

"Good to hear, Lieutenant. And I'm sure you mean well. But I need to be sure. This project is too important. Besides, do you know how hard it was to find a programmer of your caliber?"

"Thank you, Sir. I understand." *He actually smiled at me when he said that!*

Standing, to better pace behind his desk, "I'm not sure you do, Drukner. You came to us, as part of Project Millennium. The team that updated the computer and automated systems that run this base. You were such a stand-out, that I stuck my neck out for you, recommending you personally for Lead Programmer on Pinpoint. You're a top performer, and I need all of my programmers at the top of their game."

"Sir?"

Westbank stared at her for a moment, seeming to look right through her, evaluating her. "As I said, I'm not without heart. And I've given this a lot of thought. If any of my programmers are falling behind, making mistakes, or not making their quotas, I've decided it would be best to get them the help they need, rather than spend the time and resources replacing them.

"That said, I'm recommending that you report to Captain Spacer immediately, rather than waiting until the end of your shift today. She'll be able to assess the situation and make a recommendation on the best course of action." He turned to his filing cabinet, pulling out the second drawer.

"But, Sir. I think I just-"

"Immediately, Lieutenant. That's an order. Dismissed," he threw over his shoulder, already immersing himself in his next task.

That's all I need, is a frickin' head-shrinker, she thought, as she saluted and left her CO's office.

*   *   *   *   *   *

Captain Spacer's waiting room, typical of most military clinics, spoke volumes. It spoke of sterility and cleanliness, as much as it spoke of boredom: white walls, ugly flooring, metal chairs with green padding, and low tables with outdated home magazines.

Lou almost started visibly, when she noticed one of the green chairs held a man in a green uniform, suddenly jumping to his feet to salute. He was sitting so still, and so straight, that she'd missed him at first glance. "At ease, Sergeant Major. Good morning," said warmly.

"Good morning, Ma'am."

"Please, sit, Sergeant Major. I didn't mean to disturb you."

"Ma'am?"

"You…seemed deep in thought. I didn't mean to interrupt. I'm Lt. Drukner, by the way," she said politely, noting that, although he'd sat down, he hadn't relaxed in the slightest. To most, Gregory TwoDogs made for an imposing figure. He stood several inches over six feet, with the fitness level of an Olympic athlete. But his Native American features, typically serious demeanor, and a tendency to stillness created an impression that scared most people. In combat, his naturally still disposition translated to an ability to freeze in place for hours on end. Coupled with his diverse skill sets and sharp, strategic mind, and he even scared some of the men on his own Ranger team.

"Thank you for the consideration, Ma'am. I have a while to wait, and I was just praying, Ma'am. And, um…Sergeant Major Gregory TwoDogs, Ma'am," he said, introducing himself. *So, he is human after all. I was getting worried,* Lou thought with an internal chuckle.

"It's just the two of us here, and I have to confide that I'm really nervous right now," She said, sitting down in a chair on his right so that they were facing the same direction. "I've got an appointment in a few minutes, but I've never talked to a psychologist before. Could we talk, just you and I, for a bit? It might help me over the jitters."

Although it was obviously not natural to him, Lou noticed as he forced himself to relax. *Oh, my! This must not be easy for him. He's even trying to smile. How sweet.*

"If you don't mind my asking, what were you praying for?" she asked gently.

"For, Ma'am? I wasn't praying for anything in particular. I was mainly reflecting on my studies from this morning and talking to God about how it may apply to things. You pray much, Ma'am?"

"Please call me Lou when it's just you and me, okay? Like most women these days, I really don't...." She let it trail off, changing the subject instead. "To answer your question, no. I don't guess I pray very much lately. Not since...." Again, she trailed off. *Not doing so well, am I?* "What're you studying?"

He turned his face to her for the first time to say, "The Bible. What else would I...." It was his turn to trail off, in embarrassment, as he realized he'd been thinking too narrowly. *Of course, you could talk to God about any type of subject matter about how it applied to life. Duh!* He told himself accusingly.

As he quickly turned back to face forward again, Lou's mind finally wrapped itself around what she'd just seen. Almost the entire left side of Gregory's face was lined and patched with wicked scar tissue. Apparently, it wasn't enough to interfere with his duties, but it left her with flashbacks to that old opera her Grammy used to watch. *It must be why he doesn't feel comfortable enough to look at me when we talk.*

The next few minutes they spent together, Gregory told her about the Bible passage he'd read that morning and the things he'd noticed this time around, that he hadn't the other three times he'd read the same passage in the last 10 years.

Lou was surprised that anyone took reading the Bible so seriously, that wasn't a pastor, but was pleased that he took such an honest interest in it. TwoDogs was happy just to share this with someone who listened so well. *All the guys I work with, and even Dr. Spacer, never seem to want to talk about this stuff. He thought.*

*   *   *   *   *   *

Lou couldn't help looking around the room in wonder, while she and Captain Spacer made small talk. As much as the waiting room said military hospital, Spacer's office shouted Manhattan. The psychologist had gone to a lot of trouble to make her small office look like the plush, classic room one might expect to find in downtown Manhattan: dark wood furniture, leather seating, dim lighting, walls painted a tasteful dulled butterscotch with dark green accents. But to Lou, the office spoke three words, "Trying Too Hard."

Spacer tried to get her new patient to relax, as the conversation turned to her dreams. Dr. Spacer, drawing from her study of dreams in school, answered Lt. Drukner's questions as best she could. It was obvious the Lieutenant's dreams were causing the distraction Major Westbank described in his memo. But the doctor just couldn't understand why. She made a note to herself, to look up some of her old textbooks and references, once this session was over. She needed to brush up if she was going to stay ahead of this one.

"So, Lieutenant. Tell me about these dreams, then. Do your dreams normally bother you?" asked Dr. Spacer, referring to her notes.

"Well, not exactly. I usually have regular dreams, like almost everyone. But lately, things have changed."

"And this started when?" Dr. Spacer made a mark by one of her scant notes.

"About a week or so ago? I've been kind of afraid to go to sleep, so I've been staying up later than normal."

"And that's caused your attention to waver. Has it? Perhaps I should write you a prescription – on a limited basis, of course. Do you think having something to help you sleep might help?"

"No," She said quickly. "No, thank you, doctor. I wouldn't want anything that might dull my senses during the day. Besides, I'm so tired, I don't think I'll be able to keep staying up, anyway.

Am I just over-generalizing, or do doctors always seem to throw pills at everything that doesn't have an easy answer?

Spacer paused to write something, before saying, "Hmm, I see. Let's talk about these new dreams you've been having." Dr. Spacer said gently. In the quiet office, Luvenia could hear a slight whistle, from air being pushed through the vents, by conditioners.

"Well, these dreams are different. Disturbing. They don't have the disjointed quality most dreams have. Which is odd enough. But they are also sequential."

"Sequential? How do you mean?"

"Well. You know how some dreams recur, or certain elements repeat – usually because you've got something on your mind, something bothering you, right? Well, these dreams are sequential – one follows another, like pages of a book or an afternoon soap opera. Each one follows the last, building on it."

"Yes. I see. That does seem a bit different. And you think the dreams each night flow into a larger story?"

"Yes," relieved she was finally getting the idea.

"Well, that doesn't seem so bad." To herself, she said, *Sequential dreams? Who ever heard of that? She must be making it all up. This couldn't be anything to lose sleep over, certainly.*

"But that's not the strangest part, Doctor. What happened in my dreams…. It's just so terrible," Luvenia said, starting to get a bit more agitated than she wanted. "In regular dreams, it's stuff from out of your subconscious, right? But this stuff is horrible. How can I have anything like it in my head?"

"Please explain," Dr. Spacer said, noticing the Lieutenant's alarming shift in attitude. Lt. Drukner was obviously upset about something. If she could just get her to open up, they would have something to work on.

"I- I just can't. I can hardly think about it. I don't know if I could explain it."

"Please try. Take your time."

Struggling to explain, Louvenia realized the task was beyond her ability, as well as something that threatened to break her open in front of the base psychologist. *Oh, crap! I just can't. She's going to think I'm crazy. What if she has me taken off the project?* "I'm sorry. I just can't seem to put it into words," she finally dragged out.

"It's okay. Really," the Captain said as she rose from her chair and stepped over to a cabinet, secretly relieved to be able to put off discussing it further, so that she could study up on the subject. Puffing herself up, to emulate as much authority as she could, "I think the key to your current anxiety is linked to the dreams you're having, but I can't help you if I don't know anything about them. So, I'm going to give you a homework assignment of sorts."

Just as Lou realized Dr. Spacer's recent demeanor and speech pattern reminded her of a matronly school teacher, the doctor pushed something into her hands. Lou absently looked at the book the Doctor handed her. Flipping through it, she saw that it was one of those composition books she'd hated to have to use back in High School - 100 blank, lined pages. "I want you to write it all down, as best you can. Just start anywhere, and tell the story. It will be good for you to get it out and put it on paper. Tell me all you remember, and update it each morning." Then, her pleasant tone oddly turning sickly sweet, "I think this will give us both a better understanding."

Responding to the dubious look that crossed the Lieutenant's features, Spacer pinched her features into a matronly caricature of seriousness, "I'm afraid I have to insist on this. I cannot help if you won't share it with me. Trust me. Journaling is very therapeutic. Just take it a little at a time, and we'll meet again later in the week. Okay?"

Numbly, Lt. Luvenia Drukner walked out of Captain Spacer's office. *How did I get roped into THIS? I HATE writing!*

CHAPTER 7

Lou sat in her bunk, thinking about how to start her new journal. Several times, she'd thought she knew what to write, then chickened out as soon as her pen reached the paper. *Urgh! This is stupid! Why couldn't I have just kept it together? Major Westbank – Major Slave-driver, if you ask me!*

Write down the dreams. Start anywhere. So, I guess I start at the beginning, with the first one. But I just don't know if I can.

She tried again, focusing on the first dream, trying to recall how it started. And again, she stopped herself, just as the pen touched down. *No.* she thought. *This may get me in trouble, but she wants honesty. So, I'll give her honesty. There's something I have to get out first.*

This time, her pen took off, almost flying across the page, as she let out her feelings....

Entry 1:
First of all, this is a stupid assignment – a stupid idea. The only reason I'm doing this is to satisfy my superior officer's idea of helping me to cope with my stress. He's the one that set me up with Dr. Spacer in the first place. Good thing what I write won't get past the shrink, because, if I'm gonna do anything, it's tell the world what a lousy idea this is!

I've been having dreams. Weird, horror-movie dreams. Imagine looking through the eyes of Darth

Vader, while he goes about killing and enslaving (and all the "Dark Side" business he does in those old movies). It's like that.

And they run like a movie, too! Events don't repeat, like dreams sometimes do. They progress. And that's what makes it WEIRD. I don't know if anybody has ever had dreams like this - ever!

So, Doc's got me writing it down. She's nice and all, pretty for an older woman. But journaling? Really?! Whatever. I'll give it a try.

Louvenia hooked the pen to a group of inside pages, closed the journal, and threw it to the floor near her bed. *There. Its started. I'm done for today, though. Screw this stupid nonsense.*

The next morning, she tried again. Picking it up off the floor, she repeated something her sister used to tell her when there was an unpleasant job that had to be done, *Nothing to it, but to do it.* This made her laugh, remembering the way she always hated getting dirty.

Certain chores, such as taking out the trash, always upset Lou. In fact, anything that required a person to get their hands dirty qualified for Lou's best performances, trying to get out of having to do it. Trash cans were the worst. "Just hold your breath when you take off the lid, put it in quickly, and then go wash your hands. How hard can that be? Remember: There's nothing to it, but to do it. "

"But it stinks so bad. I can't hold my breath that long, Emily." Lou huffed. "If it's so easy, you do it. I'm not doing it. It's too disgusting."

"Louvenia Marie Drukner." Lou hated when her sister tried pulling out the mother card, calling her by her full name. "Get your little butt back in the kitchen, tie up the trash bag, and take it outside to the cans!"

Lou fumed, as Emily stood there watching to make sure her sister complied. "Why must we go over this every darn time? You take the bags to the cans, and I take the cans to the curb and back. It's only fair!" she said, as Lou slid angrily past her. Then, from the doorway, she added, "And make sure you put the lids back on, or the raccoons will get into them and make a mess we both will have to clean up."

Emily was right. Lou said to herself. *The hardest part of any dirty job is the procrastination. Drawing out an uncomfortable task only made the job worse.* Looking at the clock ticking away the minutes, she said to herself, *Nothing to it, but to do it, yes? Well, all right. Here goes nothing.*

Entry 2:
I really don't like this. I'm not a writer. That's why I got into computers and joined the Air Force in the first place. Being a programmer, the only writing I do is lines of code. Well, I guess I also went in to get out from under my older sister, but that's something else altogether.

Okay, that sounds bad – and really mean. It's not like that, though. She took care of me since I was 12 when our parents died. We moved in with our grandmother, but that was really just for show – Grammy didn't actually take care of us much. My sister stepped up, taking responsibility for the two of us instead and almost had to quit school. She'd had straight A's and scholarships galore, too. If it weren't for me.... Well, I just tried not to be a burden.

> After high school, I joined up and started pushing myself up the ladder. A few years later, when she had her accident...
>
> I'll have to write more about that later. Besides, I have to get ready for duty.
>
> (Ha-ha! I ran out of time!)

"We're just opening up, Ma'am. What can we do for you?"

"Coffee, Corporal. I heard you made the best cup around, so I've come to taste for myself." Louvenia said with a friendly grin after returning his salute.

Behind the counter, Corporal Blake froze awkwardly. "Well, that depends, Ma'am. I mean. No offense. It's just that, although I do make the best ground around underground," he said smiling again, "you'll have to talk to the boss about the rest. He's not too keen on word getting out about my coffee, you see." Leaning in conspiratorially, Blake said in a stage whisper, "I think he's afraid top brass will steal me away."

For some reason, the armory had a waiting area about half the size of Dr. Spacer's. Two chairs and one low table were situated on one wall, allowing access to the heavy-looking counter that ran across most of the far wall. The counter ended at a doorway to the rest of the offices, range, and secured storage.

Lou smiled brightly at that. "I understand, Corporal. It wouldn't be the first time something like that happened. So where is this boss? Shouldn't the two of you be opening up the armory together?"

"Oh, he's here, Ma'am. He came in just after you did." Blake turned to his left, gesturing. Filling the doorway, frozen at attention, stood a man with a natural demeanor that scared even the bravest of men.

How did I not notice? She thought, startled. *Oh, yes. Army Rangers are fricking Ninjas!* Recovering quickly, she said, "Good to see you again, Sergeant Major. I wasn't aware you ran our armory. I just came by to… um."

"Sign up for shooting classes. Yes. I heard." Turning to his assistant, "Corporal, do get the Lieutenant the proper forms to fill out, while I show her around the workroom. Thank you." Then to Louvenia, "This way, Ma'am. We're very proud of our setup here. I think you'll find my crew keeps everything organized and clean. Our workroom should be more comfortable than sitting out in the waiting area."

Lou suddenly realized the price for tasting Blake's coffee. But this was such a different side to the Sergeant. It intrigued her enough she decided she had to see more. At that moment, too, she decided she and Sgt. TwoDogs might learn to become friends. He was different but interesting. *Maybe I'll take him up on those shooting lessons, too.*

She listened as Master Sergeant TwoDogs talked while they enjoyed their coffee. *Yes. He's definitely loosened up a bit, now that we aren't both dreading a visit with Captain Spacer. And, damn, if this really isn't the best coffee!* Gregory TwoDogs told her about the way his armory ran, the duties it performed, the schedules it kept. He told her about Corporal Blake, his coffee, and his function. And he told her about the benefits of well-taught shooting instruction. And, although he never quite faced her directly, he smiled as he spoke. At first, Lou thought he was just trying to be polite and less scary. But she saw the light in his eyes as he spoke, showing how much he enjoyed sharing this with her.

Later, as she handed the short stack of forms over to the corporal, Lou commented, "Your boss is a rather warm guy. Not nearly as scary as he seems at first. And who knew he could smile so nicely?"

Corporal Blake looked at her oddly, "You mean Master Sergeant TwoDogs? That boss?"

"Yes, of course. Who else would I be talking about?"

"Begging your pardon, Ma'am. But I've never seen TwoDogs smile. Ever. Under any circumstances. And who would, after what he went through, right?" Corporal Blake caught himself too late. Then seeing the questioning look, he went on, "The Master Sergeant's last mission involved a helicopter accident that caused those scars you see on his face. Messed up his face pretty bad, messed up his chances to ever go out on any more missions, and maybe messed up his head a bit, too. The guy's as solid as they come, though. And I like working for him. He's always serious and by the book all day long. But he never demands of us anything he wouldn't do himself. As long as we take care of business, he pretty much leaves us to ourselves."

"Thank you, Corporal," Lou said, as she turned to leave. At the door, she turned and walked back, facing him straight on. Then, using her best 'command' voice, "Although I appreciate the insight, Corporal Blake, I do hope you aren't the type to share that sort of information about a superior, with just anyone that walks in here. Good day to you."

Lou didn't mean to be harsh, but she had a feeling any Army Ranger worth his salt would have ears like radar. Besides, it really wasn't nice to share so freely about another person like that, even if she was very curious. The corporal seemed like an okay guy, and she didn't want him to accidentally get into trouble. *Too bad Jenny won't take that advice!* She thought to herself as she walked down the hall.

Entry 3:
Third entry, and already I'm sick of numbering this stuff. Hope nobody gets bent out of shape, but I don't know if I'm gonna continue doing that.

Anyway, this journal thing is mainly about my dreams – for recording them and keeping them straight.

I may have said this before, but these dreams are different. Most are from one particular perspective, as if I'm seeing through another person's eyes (a guy's eyes – weird, right?). But more than that. I can't exactly hear, but I know what he's thinking – which is how I know he's a guy, not a girl.

Some of my dreams seem like they might be HIS dreams, or, more likely, his memories. Except he'd have to either be centuries old or reincarnated. And since the dreams seem to come in sequence, in real-time, the next dream is the next night. I'll try to go in order, from the beginning, but no guarantees.

Dr. Spacer tells me a person's memory is like that anyway; you mainly recall the highlights, then, as you hit these, maybe more details come out later. And, sometimes, they come forward out of order and have to be reorganized. Anyone who's done any interrogation knows this, too. (I watch a lot of cop shows, okay?) It's one of the reasons they make a suspect go over the story several times. It isn't just to find the holes, it's also to get the details that surface later, so they can put together a decent timeline.

The first dream was odd, but I remember the beginning for a different reason. I've never done anything in my dreams, I wouldn't do awake.

CHAPTER 8

Three entries done, and I still haven't written anything about the dreams. Idiot! I just need to get it done. Having sufficiently berated herself for her lack of discipline, Lou picked up her journal and began.

Entry 4:

I remember the first out-of-the-ordinary dream. It was hazy and shocking, disconnected too, so it's difficult to write down.

It started in a darkness that was frayed at the edges. More than the darkness, though, was a feeling of great need or thirst. It was this feeling that set it apart from anything I'd experienced before.

Understand that, as part of Basic Training, I've been beyond tired, beyond thirsty, beyond hungry, and beyond cold or hot. But, somehow, those were nowhere near what I felt in that first dream. It was a yearning, I guess is the best word for it. There was both a physical weakness that yearned for health, as well as a greedy hunger that yearned to be satisfied.

Imagine owing a mob boss hundreds of thousands of dollars. He's going to torture and kill you because you can't pay him back. Then you see enough money, all within your reach, to not only pay him back, plus interest, but to live like royalty, as well, never having to worry about money ever again. If you can imagine this, now multiply it by a million. THAT's how it was, how extreme the feeling.

<Got duty now. More later>

She knew she'd only had a few minutes, but she'd been so immersed in her writing, that she almost reported in late. All through her shift, although trying to remain focused. She kept coming back to the journal and how she would put down what came next.

*   *   *   *   *   *

Tuminov had just prized off the top of the crate, when he noticed odd sounds and voices coming from the den, just outside his office doors. Turning, he opened them to find his wife struggling in the arms of a dirty young man in overalls. Standing on either side of them, near the plush leather couch, were two others, one huge and one skinny, both dressed similarly to his wife's attacker, both just as filthy.

"Vot are you doing? Unhand my wife this instant, you *grtaznyy krest'yanin* (filthy peasant)!" Tuminov shouted indignantly. He wasn't the protective or violent type, but Hollywood had taught him the habit of throwing his weight around and making demands in such a manner that it looked like all hell was about to break loose. And the technique had rarely let him down before.

Beau and Cody cowered at Tuminov's loud, commanding tone, both turning to Austin, to suggest that it might be better if, perhaps they left, when Austin threw Bonnie into Cody and pushed Beau aside.

Striding up to Tuminov, as if he owned the place, Austin pushed his face down into the director's reddened, pudgy one, forcing Tuminov to realize he might have just used the wrong approach. "Well, that don't sound too neighborly. Does that sound neighborly to you, Beau?" he asked, glancing briefly over his shoulder at his larger brother.

"Naw, Austin. And we's just bein' friendly and all."

"Yeah, yeah. We's just bein' friendly, Austin. Just bein' friendly. Haw haw hee," Cody managed, trying to keep Mrs. Tuminov from struggling out of his arms. It'd been impossible to get free of the first one's grasp, and she feared being given over to the big one. But, having been thrown to the skinny one, she thought her odds had just improved. Bonnie struggled even harder, not counting on Cody's wiry muscles. *It's like being tied up in the branches of a tree. I can move the branches, but can't get loose from the tree.*

"I guess the big city didn't teach our fat little host much in the way of manners. Neighbors should welcome folks what's come to visit," Austin pushed Tuminov back into the office, making him stumble. Tuminov kept his feet, but kept having to back-pedal, as Austin stepped up and pushed him again and again. A few feet from the crate, Austin stopped, allowing the little man to steady himself.

"Please. I am sorry," Tuminov said very seriously. "I wish no harm or offence. Please don't..."

"Aw, I'm getting' tired of this!" Austin said as he suddenly stepped towards the director and shoved with his full strength. Tuminov pitched backwards, falling into the crate, breaking it beneath him. He felt the metal spires of the reliquary dig into his back, through the straw packed around it.

At the sight of her husband being hurt, Bonnie finally let out her first scream. More frightened for him than herself, and due to her passive nature, it somehow hadn't occurred to her to raise her voice. But now that it was clear how easily they could hurt her Toomie, her only thought was to bring their attention back to herself. No matter what that meant for her, she had to protect her man.

Cody clamped a hand over her mouth, allowing her to wiggle an arm free. But before she could use it to scratch at his eyes, Austin walked over and punched her in the gut. Bonnie felt the bile coming up, as she folded in half. Cody allowed her to collapse to the floor, laughing at his older brother's performance. *Austin's always such a sharp guy. Always knows what to do.*

"Pick her up, Beau. We're gonna have us some fun! Cody. Why don't you help our little miss out of that dress, will you? It looks so tight and uncomfortable."

"Tight and uncomfortable. Yep. That it do, Austin. Looks real uncomfortable to me, too. Haw haw hee." As Beau effortlessly picked Bonnie up from the floor, she found she had no strength. Her stomach was like jelly, and it was all she could do not to vomit all over herself.

As Beau held her up, Cody ripped at her outfit, tearing it off in pieces, as the synthetic fabric resisted. Bonnie sagged, becoming as limp as she could in Beau's grip, trying to make it harder for him to hold her, hoping the Willis boys wouldn't do what she knew they intended.

"Playin' rag doll, are ya?" Austin slapped her face with the back of his hand, causing her lip to split and swell. "That's fine by us." Turning his face to Beau's, "Remember that hitchhiker we picked up on the way back from Bixby that one time? We had such fun with her out in the old barn."

"I remembers. I remembers. She tried playin' wiggle and fight the first day, but I guess she thought we liked that too much. So, after that, she tried playin' ragdoll. She weren't very good at it. See? I remembers, Austin."

"Yeah," Austin said, putting his face up to Bonnie's. He looked at her close as if studying her features. She thought he was close enough, and was just about to bite him, when he said, "Too bad she decided to bite ol' Beau. After he hit her, playin' ragdoll was about all she was good fer. You should have seen him, Miss. He was so mad, Cody and I had to pile on him 'till he calmed down. You remember that, Beau?"

"Yessum, I do, Austin. I remembers every time we get one that wants to play wiggle and fight. But I keeps my temper better now."

"Sure. Sure. He keeps his temper better now, Austin. He does. Yeah."

"So, you play what you like. We're real accommodating. Wiggle and fight or ragdoll? We don't care which. We'd much rather you played nice with us, be a bit more neighborly and such. Yeah," he said as he ran his hand gently over her shoulder and behind her back, unclasping her bra, so that it fell to the floor, exposing her ample chest. "Now just relax and get into it, like a good host, and we won't have any--"

Just then Tuminov, clothes torn and blood dripping down his back, came rushing into the room, swinging a golf club over his head, cursing at them in Russian. The Willis boys had been so intent upon the reveal of Bonnie's voluptuous body, that they'd completely forgotten about her husband. The first to react, Cody dove for Tuminov's legs, wrapping himself around them. Then, as Tuminov refocused on the new target, Beau grabbed the club from out of his grasp. Tuminov tumbled over, falling at Austin's feet.

"You're not bein' neighborly. I've had enough of you not bein' neighborly," said Beau, bending to pick Tuminov up. Beau lifted the fat man onto his shoulder and looked around. Bonnie froze, as she saw the big man focus on the broken crate in her husband's study. He walked towards it, lifted her little Toomie, almost to the ceiling, and threw him down into the jagged pieces of wood. She gasped, unable to speak. Her husband's broken body impaled on the object within the crate, as Beau, lost in momentary fury raised his foot and stomped on Tuminov's chest, breaking ribs, as well as the reliquary hidden beneath him.

Blood soaked the packing straw, soaked the wood of the crate, and soaked the carpet. What no one could see, however, was the football-sized object hidden inside the golden reliquary had broken open, too. And it, too, was soaked with Tuminov's blood. The ancient rosewood and white oak box, splintered under the force of the impact, exposing its contents to the thick, red liquid that had only moments before, pumped through the director's veins.

The heart held within the box, kept secret in the reliquary, and safe on holy ground, beat with life once again, feeding on the fresh blood of a dying man. It grew the arteries and veins first, and reached out with them, like tendrils, sucking up the still warm blood. As it fed, it grew, and as it grew stronger, it fed more. It sucked the blood from the carpet, from the packing straw, and from the wood. It sucked the blood from the broken reliquary and shards of the smaller box. Then it found the man perched atop the pile.

Seeing her love and hope thrown down so violently, callously, and easily, then kicked so hard. Bonnie was sure her little Toomie was gone. And, with her lifeline cut so abruptly, Bonnie knew she was finished, too. All Tuminov's wealth couldn't possibly keep her alive without him, without her husband. As petty and selfish as he was, she loved him more than her own life.

Reaching up to Austin's face, she gently turned it towards herself. "I can be neighborly. It's okay. I'll be good." Austin stood agape, as she removed the last remnants of her dress and started to take off her panties. Outside, she was playing one of the old parts from one of the old movies. Inside, she was dead, and she knew it. *I just have to play the part. Not let them see,* she thought.

Entry 5:
So, last entry I was trying to describe the extreme yearning/thirsting/hunger this first dream started with. Don't know if you can relate to it, but it gets worse. The craving was for blood; a bleeding body passed out from his injuries, lying on the floor. The guy was all scratched and battered like he'd been beaten and thrown through a plate-glass window. Once I had fed enough to regain some strength, I noticed some commotion. (Yes. I use the word 'I,' because I'm seeing through someone else's eyes. I don't know who he is or what to call him. He must be some sort of monster, though, feeding on blood like that. Anyway, because of the perspective, I have to say, 'I.' Just know it's NOT me. Okay?) Three guys were arguing and shoving each other. They were the ones that had beaten the bleeding

guy 'I' was feeding on, and were now fighting over which one would go first on a woman, that must have been the bleeding guy's wife.

She crouched on a sofa, whimpering and bleeding at the lip where she'd been struck. I think she was crying for her husband more than herself or the impending rape. But I can't be sure.

I noticed these things, but, at the same time, I didn't notice anything at all. I only craved the blood and the new strength it was giving me. Also, it was as if the violence against the woman was inconsequential. Anyone else might have thought, "At least it's not happening to me." Or "This is terrible. I have to put a stop to it." But these thoughts were more like, "These men are worth nothing to me, and the woman even less. What they do to each other is of no consequence. I need to feed." No shock or care about what they were doing to that poor woman!

At this point, I woke up in a cold sweat, panting hard. It was at least another hour before I could get back to sleep.

Lou smiled to herself. She was doing well. *Maybe I should take this with me so that I can work on it at lunch. Yes. That might be a good idea, at least this once. I do have to catch up on more than a week's worth of dreams.*

Entry 6:

The rest of that night's dream was no better than its beginning. By the time 'I' finished draining the bleeding man of his blood, the three guys had finished and left, probably taking with them everything that wasn't nailed down, on their way out.

'I' saw the woman, lying face-up on the couch with a dazed look on her face. Covered in bruises and cuts, her face swollen, she turned her head and stared at 'me.' A look crossed her face, almost like lust or desire, mixed with a more obvious "who are you" look, that faded quickly, with a new wave of pain. 'I' approached her, lifting her to her feet. She stood there shaking, staring into "my" eyes.

The next part is strange. It's almost too weird to describe, but, what the hell? It's a dream, right? So anything can happen. How do I describe it, except that 'I' stood there for a moment, holding her shoulders, so she could stand. 'I' needed to know where 'I' was, and the answers were found looking in her eyes, staring in at her soul. Then, once the answers had been found, the hunger took over again and 'I' swung my hand at her head with a motion so fast it seemed only a blur, ripping her head clean off of her body. I could feel 'my' mouth opening like a snake's, further than a human should be able. And, before her body could fall or more than a single spurt of blood could hit the ceiling, 'I' lifted her up, so that 'I' could drink from her like someone might do from a soda bottle!

(Where does my imagination come up with stuff like this?!!!)

Anyway. After that, when 'I' was done, 'I' set fire to the house and traveled towards the lights of the town. (Okay. Now I say "traveled," but the person I was looking out of, didn't exactly walk or run. 'I' rolled over terrain and flowed towards the town, like a mist or fog, rather than a car or glider.

The first business had the brightest lights. Fennel's Hardware had closed a few hours earlier. But 'I' could perceive there were people inside – probably stocking the shelves. 'I' headed there with the idea of help. Well, maybe "allies" might be a better word.

I remember a smirking thought as 'I' glided past some "WELCOME" mats, stacked beside the front door. But I'm not sure why 'I' did this.

<An emergency call has come in from Command. More later.>

CHAPTER 9

"Well, the first part is a little unexpected. But I'm glad you were honest and took this assignment seriously. Many people do have obstacles to freeing up their writing, so we'll just put it down to that sort of thing, shall we?" Lou could tell Dr. Spacer was upset that she'd been so overly candid in writing down how she felt. She'd been pushing her luck, hoping that the doctor wouldn't tell Major Westbank. Luckily, Spacer wasn't the type to tattle. A notation would go into her records, of course. But the odds of anyone significant reading that report, and it's being held against her were slim.

"Let's focus on just this first dream. You explain in your journal that it's like seeing through someone else's eyes, that it isn't you that's doing these things. So let's assume, for now, it isn't you. Tell me how you felt about the things you witnessed."

*   *   *   *   *   *

When she was by herself again, Louvenia decided something a bit out of the ordinary just might be in order. Raised in a Christian home, she'd been to church every Sunday. Even after she joined the Air Force, she kept up the tradition. She'd even accepted Jesus into her heart at age nine. If asked, she would answer that, yes, she was born again. But if she was honest with herself, she would have to admit she didn't have a very close relationship with God.

Although she still went to church, at least a few times a month, she rarely prayed. Emily had given her a brand new Bible when she'd enlisted, and Lou still had it in pristine condition, still wrapped in its original plastic wrapper.

She felt like God was there, where He has always been, overseeing and protecting. But felt she was so far away from Him like the world was carrying her further and further away. Right now, though, she needed to open up to someone that understood, someone she knew would listen, someone that wouldn't think her crazy, and maybe someone that might help her.

"Oh, dear, Lord," she said, glancing up at the ceiling. "This journaling stuff seems like it's coming easier, now that I've gotten started. And it might really help me, too, just to get the details on paper. But these sessions with Dr. Spacer," she said as tears welled up with frustration. "I hope they aren't all like this one. *'How did this make you feel?'* Awful. *'How did that make you feel?'* Terrible. *'What about this other thing?'* Disgusted!

How many different ways can I say it, Lord?!! Awful, terrible, disgusting. Urgh! Ghastly, horrible, appalling, atrocious, horrendous, frightful, revolting, sickening. Double urgh!

"I'm not sure I can do any more of this, if our sessions just keep dragging over the same ground, over and over again! That was the longest hour I've ever had to endure." Lou caught herself pacing, journal still in hand. She'd been about to throw it across the room, but caught herself.

"I just need strength, Lord. I've just never had dreams like this before. They're terrible! I mean, I'm fascinated, curious I guess, about the story that's unfolding. But it's scaring the hell out of me. Am I going crazy? I don't want to end up going on some sort of killing spree or end up locked away, in a padded cell, either.

"Please help me, Lord. You're the only one that can do anything about this. As much as I want to be in control, I can't control my dreams. You've got to help me!

"Look. I don't want to be all nitpicky here, but how does this work into your plan? Is this supposed to teach me something? Maybe you could toss me a clue or something.

"I don't know. I just need your help. I can't do this by myself. If this has to go on any longer, please give me the strength to endure it. And help me out when I meet with Dr. Spacer, too, if you don't mind. We're supposed to meet next week, so...

"Thanks. Thanks for listening.

"In Jesus' name, Amen."

As she blew her nose and cleaned her face, she realized she felt a lot better, comforted by giving her problems over to a higher power. Taking the journal over to her bed, she decided to write a bit more before turning in for the night.

Entry 7:
Shortly after my last entry, I remembered something about that woman. As she and 'I' faced each other (before 'I' killed her, of course), 'I' stared into her eyes and knew, I mean KNEW her thoughts. They were open to 'me,' like a library – a front display of current thoughts, backed by rows and rows of books. And each of these books, memories and learned knowledge. 'I' stepped past the display of current thought, reached past her life memories, and took from her a base knowledge: memories of language, reading, speech, our society, and how things work. Her knowledge was rather minimal, limited to the experiences of the life of an aspiring actress, I guess. But that was all 'I' was after.

Anyway, to finish that first dream, 'I' entered the hardware store, flowing through the cracks in the door. 'I' was completely unnoticed, until 'I' found the closing manager. This was the ally 'I'd' been looking for. Don't ask me how. The person I was looking through was just able to see into him and read the guy's type. His name tag read Dwight Wendis, easily readable, as it was polished to a high shine, reflecting how important he thought he was, as well as how little actual work he did. He was the kind of guy that reveled in abusing his limited power. The kind that turned his sweetest face to the boss, then pushed those under him around when the boss wasn't there. He craved power and prestige but was frustrated because he could not prove himself more capable. (Typical small-minded, middle-management bully!) But he could be seduced by an offer of more power – the kind 'I' could use.

My alarm woke me up at that point, so I don't know what happened next. I guess 'I' asked this guy to help, maybe. There was a fear about the light that was on its way (maybe daylight?), but I don't know.

She put her pen down and closed the journal over it, relieved, not only that she'd finally gotten started, but that she'd done much better writing it down than she thought she would. It kind of flowed out. And, once on the page, she felt a weight lift from her.

CHAPTER 10

Louvenia woke up early the next morning, feeling focused and refreshed. After a hot shower, she sat down at the desk in her quarters, deciding to get more writing done. She felt she had to get caught up somehow. She was several days behind and wanted to get to the point where she was writing the events of the night before. *It'll be so much easier if I don't have to think so far back, to get this written down. I just hope Dr. Spacer eases up next time. Maybe, by getting caught up, she'll be able to do something other than keep dragging out all the "How does that make you feel?" questions.* Then she thought, *I wonder if there's any way I can skip out on the next session. Probably not. But I wonder if there is.* Her next session wasn't until next week. She smiled, reveling in her good luck.

She thought back to the events of the second night, making a cold shiver run through her. She shuddered, too, remembering the sadness and disgust, causing the cold sweat that had woken her up that morning.

Entry 8:

The next night was the librarian. You see 'I' needed more information; about us, how we think, how we have progressed. (Which means this guy was apparently pretty ancient. The connections he made were with things as they might have been back in the Dark Ages or something.)

The manager at the hardware store was somehow made into an ally. But the Librarian was different.

She worked the late shift, doing the majority of the grunt work, putting all the books away, and generally straightening up and cleaning. She worked alone.

With the lady 'I' killed back at the ranch, 'I' didn't bother to look at what kind of person she was. 'I' just wanted some basic knowledge (which was, for the type of person she was, all she really had to offer). When the hardware store guy was made into an "ally" (I think "minion" is probably a much better word), the whole thing was quick. One look and 'I' knew what kind of guy he was. But the Librarian was different.

'I' was there to learn (and 'I' wanted to know and understand, less out of curiosity, and more because 'I' wanted to take advantage). So, although the late-night Librarian helped facilitate that desire, she was not made an ally (minion) she was made into something different. The word that ran through 'my' mind was "thrall." And into 'my' thrall, she would be made. 'My' approach got her attention. As soon as our eyes met, her life was open to 'me':

Childhood – Only child, puzzles, play, fun, "You're so smart, Abigail, my Little Princess."

Elementary – Smartest girl in school, loved by teachers and adults of all sorts, parents so proud.

Jr High – Teachers' pet, parents even more proud of her grades and accomplishments, but noticing other kids avoid her.

High School – Still teachers' favorite, responsible, trusted by many adults in town, parents about fit to burst with pride, winning academic awards, college scholarships promised, ignored or ridiculed by peers – too lonely, boys only noticing the pretty girls (especially Lindsey Mae Atkins – dumbest girl in school), yearning for love, as much as academic respect.

College – High marks, no social life, notices guys, realizing they only noticed shapely girls, not plain, skinny nerds like her.

Back Home – Must take care of parents now, too busy to notice her loneliness.

Parents Death - Deciding to take her inheritance to get cosmetic surgery, a breast enlargement, in the city – maybe then, guys will notice her.

Returning Home – Full of hope, wearing her new contacts, happy with her new look, and smiling in her new sun dress. Shocked by the community's reaction: ridicule, scorn, shame. Nothing has changed. Decides to take the night shift at the library to avoid people as much as possible. Hiding herself under long, matronly dresses and baggy sweaters.

Yearning for love. Dissatisfaction. Disappointment. Yearning for a connection, of love, for someone of her own, attention like other girls get, belonging to another. Yearning for love....

'I' was looking past her thoughts, into her memories, and finding her true self: disappointment and yearning. THESE were what 'I' was looking for, what 'I' needed to find. These made her different, not corrupted by the need for power, but the ability to BE corrupted – to taint the otherwise innocent soul.

And, at that moment, she understood and was corrupted by her own desires and regrets, as 'we' stared into each other's eyes. This is what 'I' wanted: to get in, to find the flaw, to exploit the desire, and corrupt the soul.

As the shock and horror settled, I came to understand the blackness of the monster's soul. I felt 'my' lips on hers. The lips moved to her ear, to the lobe, and down. 'I' reveled in the thrill of the subtle, intimate contact. A slight discomfort, yet relief, as 'my' hunting teeth slid out further.

The kiss became a bite, puncturing, tearing the skin, and ripping the flesh. As 'my' bite severed the artery beneath, a rich, creamy, warm, rushing river burst itself onto 'my' lips and into 'my' mouth. 'I' drank it deep, thoughts of nourishment and savoring appreciation, like a master vintner honoring his finest wine. 'I' drank deeply, but savored every rushing, pulsing morsel that rushed over and through 'my' teeth.

His thoughts flowed. I heard them this time, as they were strong and obvious. "Yes. This was the finest and most luscious kind. True innocence? Too sweet. Evil? Bitter as bile. But tainted innocence! Yes. There is nothing to compare to tainted innocence. Corruption made for the best, and most enjoyable food."

Which is, of course, when I woke up, thinking, "Holy Crap! That was BLOOD! I was drinking a LIVE person's blood!" Well, not me, exactly. No. Not me. I had to remind myself. It wasn't me! I was seeing through someone else's eyes. It had to be someone else! His actions, words, thoughts, and even his memories, were completely foreign to me! I've never seen the things his memories dredged up – the connections he made. It couldn't be me, right? I just don't see how that monster could be me.

As Lt. Louvenia Drukner finished, she looked up at the clock. She'd been so entranced in her writing, she'd not only completely missed her time for chow, she was going to be late reporting for duty! Grabbing her cover, she bolted down the hallway, only slowing when she arrived at her office. She signed in as quickly as she could at the guard station while trying to control her breath. *Crumbs! If Major Westbank looks as closely at the log, as he does with everything else, he'll find out I was late! I totally forgot.* She walked to her desk as casually as she could, hoping not to attract attention. *Westbank is a stickler... minutes? Probably not.*

*   *   *   *   *   *

Lt. Drukner happily threw herself into her work, temporarily forgetting all about the dreams that bothered her so much. By the time lunch came, she was famished. Skipping breakfast had made her hungry enough to chew wallpaper! Leaving her desk, she saw her journal sitting on the desk. Realizing she'd accidentally taken it with her when she'd left this morning, she decided she'd take it with her to lunch again. Something was bothering her that she felt was worth writing down.

Entry 9:

I was thinking about that dream and the blood-drinking. He's got to be some kind of monster or fiend, but I refuse to call him Dracula, okay? Drinking blood is vampirism. But that doesn't mean he has a severe widow's peak, comes from Transylvania, and wears a black cape and cowl. Those movies are such silly rubbish anyway, right?

I mean sure. Real, modern-day vampires exist in America. Ha, ha, ha!

Of course, these are just dreams, right? What's happening isn't real, so it really doesn't matter.

But it SEEMS so real! I think that's what freaks me out most of all. It's not just the change from regular dreams, to those that tell a story. It's that they feel so freaking real!

Later, before turning in, she decided she wasn't quite finished explaining what was bothering her. So, instead of going to bed on time, she stayed up a little while longer. *Besides, I've made a decision, and I want Dr. Spacer to read it. Maybe she'd ease up on the "How do you feel," nonsense and focus on something else. (And maybe she'll stop giving me that "I think you're making this all up," look, too!)*

Entry 10:
I've decided not to describe this as 'I' anymore, but 'he,' because I am convinced this monster is NOT me. It couldn't be me – not even in my wildest nightmares, could I come up with something so repulsive as actually drinking someone else's blood! How could anyone?!

Which begs the question: If those dreams aren't coming from MY subconscious, where are they coming from?

This is really bothering me!

CHAPTER 11

Running hard, but breathing normally, Dwight thrilled in his new-found strength. He felt like he could lift a house off its foundations and run with it on his back, all without breaking a sweat. He turned down Everly Street, where his master confirmed Abigail lived. He had to hurry. Now that a better place had been found to keep the Master safe, he needed to get to this thrall fast. She would be turning soon, and the sunlight would kill her.

Dwight had begun walking to Abigail Quinn's house an hour or so earlier, with plenty of time to get where he needed to go. But now he had to hurry. Passing through the empty lot, near the railroad tracks, he'd smelled something, and had to investigate. The scent reminded him of a time when he was a kid.

He'd been walking by himself, along the railroad tracks, coming back from the drug store, when he ran across the Willis boys: Austin, Beau, and Cody. They decided to play together, lining up a few .22 bullets on the tracks, in time for the afternoon train. While they waited, they got to bragging and telling fibs. Austin mentioned he'd seen a dead body on the tracks, down by the bridge. Dwight accused him of lying and before they knew it, all four of them were running, as boys do, on their way to beat the old "double-dog dare," the bullets left on the track, forgotten.

Slowing to a walk and out of breath, they got to the place the Willis boys had seen the thing. As the boys approached, they swore to each other it had to be human. "Maybe it's a hobo." "I bet it's old man Atkins. He's always tyin' one on whenever he gets a few dollars." "If it is, I could go break the news to his granddaughter, Lindsey Mae." "Lindsey Mae Atkins sure is purty!" "Hell, yeah! I heard she's already wearing a bra, too."

The boys talked while walking closer and only stopped when the breeze that had been blowing across their path stopped for a few seconds. Then the smell of rotting flesh hit them. The Willis boys laughed, as Dwight retched, barely keeping himself from throwing up. They were all pinching their noses against the pungent smell. Burning with embarrassment, Dwight tried his best, but even covering his mouth didn't keep out the taste of the foul odor.

By the time they got close enough to poke the decaying mound with a stick they'd found, it dawned on them that they were looking at an animal of some kind. It had obviously been hit by the passing train, the way it was twisted and torn open. Somewhat disappointed they hadn't discovered something more important, they still thrilled in the moment. This was the first dead thing they'd ever seen that wasn't dressed, cooked, and placed on the dinner table. They'd never even been to a funeral.

So, when Dwight caught the scent near the tracks today, his mind took an unannounced trip to that memory long passed. The scent seemed the same, but something was different, and he just had to find out what that was.

He approached more boldly than his 10-year-old self had that first time, poking about, again with a conveniently located stick. As before, the wind shifted, this time straight for him, blasting him with the smell of death. This time, however, instead of choking and dry-heaving, he found his mouth watering. It still stung his nose and burned his throat to breathe in that scent, but this time something in him welcomed the invisible, formerly vomit-inducing cloud.

Dwight bent down in the pile of rubbish. His hands, as if with a mind of their own, reached for the dead cat. He marveled at the number of unnamed creatures that wriggled and writhed in and among the eyes, nose, and mouth. Fascinated, he touched the thing with his bare hand, appalled at what he was doing, but unable to stop himself.

Later, brushing himself off, he sighed in satisfaction as he licked the remnants off his lips and fingers. As good as he'd felt before, now he felt great, powerful even. He was filled with energy. Even his senses felt heightened. Glancing at his watch, however, he realized that more time had passed than he'd realized, and now he ran the risk of being late. He couldn't be late! The Master would never allow him to live if Dwight failed to protect his new thrall from the sun.

So, running hard, he came upon one of several similar houses in the neighborhood. The one he was looking for, marked with bold letters on a mailbox out front that read, "QUINN," could be easily picked out from a distance.

He stopped at the door, noting that he still wasn't breathing hard, which thrilled him. He'd never been very athletic since high school, and running flat-out like that would have left him on his knees with stomach pain, panting like a dying horse, and sweating profusely. He calmly knocked on the door, and rang the bell, just in case she'd already gone to bed. As soon as she answered her door, he remembered the shy, skinny bookish girl from his days in school. She stood there wide-eyed, looking somewhat frightened, hugging a high-collared, baggy sweater tightly to herself. *Who could be knocking at my door this early in the morning? It's my bed-time! Heck. The sun isn't even up yet, for goodness sake!*

"Mornin', Abbey. Don't mind if I call you Abbey, do ya?" he said, as he breezed past her. Before she could answer, he continued, "Sorry we don't have much time t' talk. Gotta get you some protection, b'fore sunrise."

Abigail remembered to close the door, before hurrying after him. He'd headed down the hall and disappeared into her bedroom of all places, where she could hear thumping. As she rounded the corner, something crashed. She looked in, to find her favorite bedside lamp in pieces on the floor. Dwight was throwing armfuls of clothes from the walk-in closet, across the room. One of these had snagged the lamp, toppling it to the ground.

"My clothes! What-what are you doing, Dwaine?" she stammered, mispronouncing his name on purpose. She remembered him, all too well, as one of her worst bullies and abusers in school.

"Dwight," he corrected, tossing the last armful of dresses into a corner. "Dwight Wendis, Abbey. You remember me from school? I'm the Assistant Manager of Fennel's Hardware store now," he said proudly. *Although, due to the Master's intervention, I will become much more.*

He grabbed up all the bedding and said, "Can ya hold these blankets, while I get this mattress? Thanks," as he shoved them into her hands, not giving her time to refuse. She held them close, quickly remembering to hide the bandage covering the gaping, discolored wounds she'd discovered on her neck.

As soon as she had them, he turned back to her bed, lifting the queen-sized mattress as if it didn't weigh as much as she knew it did. She remembered the way the two delivery guys grunted with effort as they carried it into her house. She stood gaping, as he folded it in half, as if it were one of her comforters, and stuffed it into her walk-in closet, of all places. But the weight, awkwardness, and difficulty of wrestling her mattress into the closet, didn't seem to bother Dwight at all.

Such a strange event, happening so fast, was so completely different from her quiet, orderly, solitary life. She was trying to form the words to ask Dwight to explain why he was doing this, when he stepped over to her, grabbing her up in his arms, blankets and all. He lifted her, as one might a child, and walked her over to the closet, setting her down on the mattress. Surprisingly, the mattress just about fit the closet perfectly.

"Now look, Miss Quinn," he said from the doorway, holding up his hands as if interrupting an argument. As she stared up at him, half shocked and half frightened, he continued, "I know this is all new to you, but ya gotta trust me. I done this for the Master, keepin' him safe and all. And he told me to do the same for you, too. So that's what I'm doin'. Just bed yerself down in here, okay? At least ya don't have to make do in a storage closet!" Forceful, but courteous, this Dwight Wendis acted completely different from the bully she remembered from school.

"Now, I'm gonna seal this here door up, so the light don't get in. It'll be plenny dark, but don' you be scared or nothin'. Changin' is kind of odd – was for me, anyways. You'll understand more when you wake up. Trust me." And, as if that explained everything, he shut the door. Stunned at the sudden events, she was reluctant to move. A minute or so later, she could hear movement on the other side of the door, followed by the banging of a hammer. By the time Dwight was done with whatever he was doing, Abigail sat in pitch darkness. Even the small band of light that usually seeped in under the door was gone.

She wanted to get up, but she was so sleepy. She wanted to check the door, but her eyes kept wanting to close. She wanted to ask more questions, to do something, anything about her confusion, but she found herself unable to rise. Although her normal bedtime was approaching, waves of drowsiness overcame her. They were like nothing she'd ever experienced before, almost as if someone had flipped a switch. She just couldn't resist it. As she clutched the wad of blankets to herself, she just…had…to sleep.

*   *   *   *   *   *

As Abigail Quinn slept, she dreamed. And as she dreamed, childhood memories came back to her. From the time Abigail entered school, she had a crush on a curly-haired boy named James-Wayne Fennel. His father had just purchased the town hardware store and moved into the house next door. She spent all the time she could with him. They walked to school together, did their homework together, and spent time talking together down by the creek. He even let her call him JW.

By junior high, she finally had the opportunity to tell him how she felt. She could ask him to the Sadie Hawkin's dance; a time when it was okay for a girl to invite a boy. But he'd already been asked by the Atkins girl. That would have been okay, but then he said the most hurtful word a girl who felt the way she did could hear: friends.

From that moment on, the space between them widened. Abigail tried her best to heal the fracture, but it was no use. Shortly after the Sadie Hawkins incident, Mr. Fennel moved his family to a nicer part of town. Abigail could blame his father's new prosperity and JW's new friends to be the cause of the bullying jerk he was today. But Lynsey Mae Adkins was the real reason. She was the wedge driven in too deep, bolstered by a circle of friends that had no patience for nerdy academics like her. Somehow, they all saw Abigail as a threat and began a campaign against her, that would follow her into adulthood.

By the time her parents died, Abigail thought the feud to be over. They were adults now. They should be able to move beyond petty childhood games and jealousies. But, when Abigail returned from the city, with her new look and contact lenses, expecting to be treated like a regular person, she only found the pettiness continued, souring most of the town against her once again. So, she did what she'd always done. She hid herself away, working the night shift at the library, trying not to be noticed.

*   *   *   *   *   *

Normally, Abigail woke a few hours before sunset, in preparation for her late shift at the library. This time, she woke late, feeling a bit strange. Standing up in her closet, hazily trying to recall the events of that morning. *Did Dwight come over, mess up my bedroom, and make me sleep in the closet? Or was I just dreaming that?*

As she pushed her way out of the closet, she found her bedroom all put back together. Except for a bed without a mattress and boards sealing her windows, it was as if it had never been disturbed.

Moving to the bathroom, Abigail froze in place. Her image in the mirror wasn't right. She could see through herself as if she were turning into a ghost! After a hot shower, she assured herself she wasn't seeing things, but she could tell that many things had changed. It wasn't just the morning's upset, sleeping in a closet, and waking up to discover she could see through herself, though. She felt significantly different as well. And the mark on her neck, she remembered discovering earlier, had completely disappeared.

"Hello, Doreen? This is Abigail. Listen. I'm sorry I'm not there already, and I know it's short notice, but I don't feel well, so I won't be in tonight, okay?" she waited for the reply, then said goodbye. Intending to stay in and figure out just what was happening to her, she found herself putting on her best dress and makeup instead. A part of her was shocked that she was acting without consciously thinking about it. Normally, she made determined, well-thought-out decisions, and never acted so impulsively. But she just couldn't find the will to stop and consider.

*   *   *   *   *   *

Abigail walked into Joe's Steakhouse, the closest thing Willow Switch had to a roadhouse bar. As she did, she could feel the people crowding the room, as if pulsing with subtle heat. Normally, she avoided places like this and would have entered with trepidation, if at all. Tonight, she moved with a grace and smoothness she hadn't known she possessed, almost flowing through the bodies packed into the place. She smiled as she felt the looks, this time favorable, rather than accusing or derogatory. It was as if they were seeing a totally different person.

Abigail's smile grew wide, as she saw the heads turn and over-heard the comments, "Will you look at that?", "Well slap my momma!", "Daaamn! Who's she?", "Don't you get to staring, Jimmy-Wayne! That's my next ex-wife!" And she marveled that she could hear them over the loud music and hubbub.

As Abigail made her way to the bar, Lindsey Mae Atkins set down a fresh round of beers at a nearby table and said, "That's $16, boys," with a wink and a smile bigger than Texas. She loved busy nights like this. Every Friday and Saturday night, she wore her shortest cut-off shorts and knotted her t-shirt a bit tighter over her padded bra, to show off her figure a bit better. These small changes made sure every eye was on her, and always earned her lots of big tips.

"I said, that's $16 guys!" she repeated. "Guys!," she huffed, not used to being ignored. *They should be handing me $20 and telling me to keep the change, not staring off into space!* Instead, one of them handed her two tens and, without so much as a glance in her direction, said, "Oh, yeah. Here you go, Lins. And send one to that hot gal that just came in, will ya?" Still staring at someone at the bar, he elbowed the guy next to him and said with a sheepish grin, "Tell her I sent it to her, 'kay?"

Math had never been her strongest subject. But having served little more than $4 beers for so long, she'd learned to think in 4's. *Wait. That would mean my tip would be…Urgh!!* Linsey screamed to herself. Rolling her eyes, she snatched up the bills and turned on her heel angrily. She stopped a few steps away and took a deep breath, pushing it out of her mind. *No. That tip's mine. Whoever she is, she can buy her own damn beer. I'm not doing nothing but going to the next table and taking the next order,* she thought, vindictively pocketing the extra money. *I deserve this tip!* "What's that, Hunny? Keep the change?" she whispered to herself with a smirk. "Why thank you, sweetheart! That's so nice of you."

Abigail continued to smile, enjoying the positive attention lavished upon her. Surrounded by men of all ages and types, buying her drinks – too many drinks, and trying to offer her cigarettes or a dance. Shortly, she realized it might be easier to say yes, but she smiled as she all but drowned under their offers and attention. She reveled in the new experience and found it difficult to select just one.

At that moment, however, she noticed the one person that would make a good night perfect. And he was making his way over. Jimmy-Wayne Fennel, spoiled-brat son of James Fennel Sr. (of Fennel's Hardware) and life-long crush since grade school. He had been the Willow Switch High School's All-Star Quarterback, Senior Class President, and Prom King. He was engaged to Injun Joe's waitress, Linsey Mae Atkins. Jimmy-Wayne had been stringing poor Linsey Mae along since they first started going together in Junior High. Funny, but all the time they'd been together, "faithful" had never been in JW's vocabulary. The saddest thing was, that everyone seemed to know of his infidelity, except the brainless Miss Atkins.

From the moment he walked over and said, "Howdy," Jimmy-Wayne was trapped. He'd noticed every other guy in the place's attention shift when Abigail walked in, causing the bantam rooster inside him to take notice. Jimmy-Wayne did not like other men to have anything if Jimmy-Wayne couldn't have it first. So, bold as brass and as cool as he could, he got up and started working his way over.

Flipping the collar of his genuine silk, Ford Mustang racing jacket, Jimmy-Wayne tried his best lines. Knowing he wasn't very good at making small talk, Abigail took pity and invited him to dance with her. The jukebox had switched to a slow one, and Abby took advantage. Part of her was motivated by revenge and part by her new-found energy. She seemed to have an unidentifiable need that went beyond desire. She was finally getting her shot at her childhood crush and most popular guy in school, and she wasn't going to let anything ruin it.

They danced just long enough for Linsey Mae Atkins to notice and begin fuming with jealousy. *Sauce for the goose.* Abby thought when Linsey begin to make her way over. Then Abby told JW how much she loved muscle cars, especially Mustangs. *Even if I hadn't known the kind of vehicle Jimmy-Wayne owned, his jacket would have made it obvious.* Like a starving trout, he jumped at the bait, wanting to get her into it. Jimmy even blushed with anticipation, as they left together.

Abby made sure to linger a moment outside, just long enough for the waitress to catch up to them. Linsey Mae yelled at Jimmy-Wayne and punched him in the chest. JW looked sheepish and tried to play it off. Meanwhile, Abby watched from the shadows near his car, acting like she didn't notice the lover's spat. Every time Linsey Mae looked over, Abby was innocently looking somewhere else. But each time Jimmy-Wayne glanced at her, all he saw was a sensuous woman leaning seductively against his car, beckoning him to come to her.

By the end of the argument, Linsey Mae threw her ring at him and stormed back inside. As the front door to the steakhouse slammed, Jimmy-Wayne picked up the ring and impotently yelled a few choice words in the direction his now ex-fiancé had gone. Then he turned, changing back to his bantam demeanor, and slowly ambled over to Abby, explaining, "She'll get over it. Always does."

From the moment Linsey Mae saw JW talking to her, Abby never doubted how the scene would play out. And she laughed to herself, as he tried to cover his embarrassment and play it cool. As soon as they were seated in his car, she turned to him, so that he would kiss her. He responded, and they made out for several minutes. Abby melted into the act of kissing. Although this was her first time, she'd dreamt of this moment with him since Junior High. Beautiful and intimate, kissing made her blood run hotter.

She noticed in herself, how she writhed and moaned under his awkward touch. She wanted more. She panted, as he ran his hands across her shoulders and under the shoulder strap of her dress. His kisses moved from her mouth to her ear, to her neck, and his hands wandered further down.

Exploding with the passion of the moment, she ran her fingers through his hair and brought his head up, staring into his eyes. They connected, as lovers connect, spirit to spirit, letting the passion flow. He kissed her lips again, and let her take her turn, working her kisses down onto his neck.

Yeah, buddy. Now this is what I'm talkin' about. Dern girl's turnin' me on big-time. Not sure the last time Linsey done anythin' like that, he thought to himself. For a moment, when she sank her teeth into his flesh, masterfully opening his jugular, the pain seemed like a distant thing. All too quickly, however, the pain rushed up, overwhelming him. The gash was wide and deep. Jimmy-Wayne let out a sharp cry of pain and tried pushing her away. "Hey! What the hell? Hey! Get offa me!" Clutching the side of his head, one hand full of curly hair, she clamped the other over his mouth, holding him fast. She inhaled his essence, drinking in the life-sustaining fluid. After a few minutes, his struggles slowed. Finally, letting out one last whimper, he lost consciousness, and death claimed him completely.

When the blood stopped pumping, and she couldn't get any more to come out, Abby pushed his body against the driver's side window and leaned back in the imitation sheepskin covering the passenger seat. She felt relaxed but energized. She felt tired but excited. Yesterday, the thought of killing a man by drinking his blood would have shocked Abigail Quinn. But the new Abby wasn't bothered by it at all. In fact, she found she no longer thought of anything the same way as before. Climbing out of the car, she turned herself to better hear the Master's subtle voice. *Yes. I will teach you more about this new perspective. But first, wait there for Dwight. He will take care of the body for you. For that is a minion's job. Then come to me, and I will teach you a Thrall's duties.*

CHAPTER 12

The next few weeks proved to be very busy for Lt. Luvenia Drukner, and she was not able to devote as much time to her journal writing, as she might have liked. Just as she'd gotten caught up, the workload for her team was increased, as the testing schedule for Project Pinpoint was moved forward. Further adding to the stress and difficulty, daily inspections by upper brass and politicians of all sorts became the norm. Major Westbank demanded daily progress reports be read to him during several meetings, and Lou was even chosen to perform last-minute assessment presentations.

Oddly enough, her nights became a bit more restful during this time, as the monster fell into something of a routine.

Entry 11:
I'm having to summarize the last few weeks, as everything really hit the fan around here. Meetings, inspections, reports, presentations – holy cats, we've been busy!

Every night, I dreamed of the monster, looking out of his eyes. He visits the library every night, waited on by his "thrall" (as he thinks of her), and feeds on victims captured and brought to him by Dwight, the minion/ally/manager. His victims usually look like they may be homeless men, but some are younger and better dressed

– people from town that won't be missed? Tourists, maybe?

With great horror, I experienced each victim. They'd be led in and terrorized, enhancing their fear, before the monster attacked. (I got the impression that either the blood tastes better injected with fear, or it would otherwise taste terrible, so fear was induced to mask it.) He always leaves something for his thrall (yes, they feed, too). Then Dwight takes out the body and cleans up, while the monster calmly returns to his studies. One time, I noticed the minion's eyes light up, as he moved to pick up a body. He was drooling hungrily. (Is he eating the dead bodies? Eew!)

The monster studies all subjects, starting with World History, moving through Engineering and Science, and finally ending with magazines on current events and business trends for the last 10 years (I noticed one was a USA Today). He reads quicker than most and is able to follow even the most convoluted authors, linking subjects and ideas at a genius level. He doesn't seem to have any trouble with languages. No matter what language the text is written in, it never slows him down. (How is it possible he is able to understand so many languages?!)

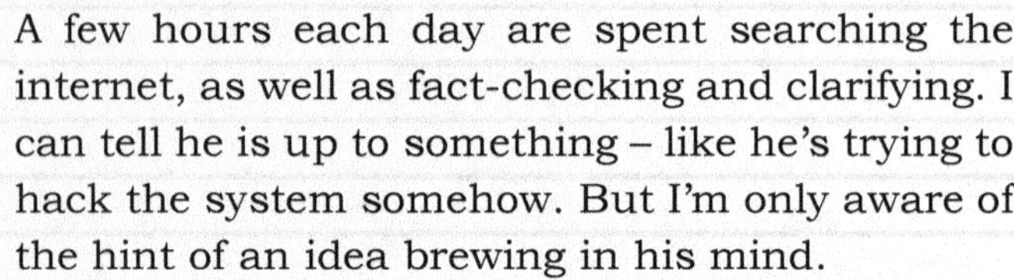

Lou woke in a sweat, gasping to breathe. *Oh, crap! That was the worst!*
She thought, feeling sick to her stomach. She threw off the covers,
vowing not to go back to sleep for a while. Looking at the clock,
however, told her she wasn't going to miss a whole lot of sleep at this
point. *Maybe I ought to start taking naps in the middle of the day, so
I don't have to see this kind of stuff,* she said to herself, knowing that
wouldn't be possible.

As she rose, she stripped off the shorts and tee she normally wore to bed,
and climbed into the shower. The hot water helped to wake her up and clear
her head. *Just figures, right? Just when I thought things were getting quiet
and boring, the monster decides to mix things up. This has to end sometime,
doesn't it? Not sure I can take much more of this if it does.*

Tempted to call Dr. Spacer, Lou decided not to bother the woman only a few
hours from the start of day shift. *Besides, she'll just hit me with more of that
"How does that make you feel?" nonsense.* Her meetings with Dr. Spacer
would have to start up again, now that the VIPs had moved on to other
departments and the workload had gone back to normal. But so far, it didn't
seem like her meetings with Dr. Spacer had really helped that much.

The Doc treated her gently and spoke very kindly, and it was obvious
she strove to be understanding. But it seemed as if these dreams were
quite out of the doctor's depth. Drukner could imagine Dr. Spacer on
the phone with her colleagues, searching through volumes of academic
papers, and reading everything she could find, trying to get a clue as to
what these dreams were about.

She wrapped herself in one towel, dried her hair on another, and padded
back into the main room, feeling better after spending time under the hot

water. Luvenia enjoyed her studio apartment, even if it was more than a mile underground. At times, it was like living in a submarine. But most of the time, residents didn't notice. The Air Force, after much research and some budgetary adjustments, had added faux windows and special day/night cycled lighting so that the place mimicked the surface world as much as possible. She had divided the main room into two sections, one for sleeping, and one as her office. Sitting at her desk, she flipped on the desk lamp for added light and opened her journal.

Entry 12:
Last night, something different happened, involving the city's Mayor. I saw him coming out of the courthouse with a woman the monster knew to be his secretary after most everyone had gone home already. (I could just make out the name of the town on the front of the building: Willow Switch.) Apparently, he and his secretary were working late, but I couldn't detect any hanky-panky had gone on between them. And she didn't seem very attractive. So maybe they really were working. (Mayor of such a small town, though.... What else could he have been doing, if not schtuping his assistant, right?)

The monster waited until the secretary had driven off, before moving towards him with his minion, cutting the Mayor off from his vehicle. The Mayor was tall and carried a slight pudginess, that somehow added to the fatherly jolliness of his face – perfect for a politician.

His Honor the Mayor (I don't know his name since it never came up in the monster's thoughts), being used to everyone in town either loving him or fearing him, was not easily intimidated. Although a bit surprised at the late hour of the monster's approach, he seemed more upset at being accosted by a stranger without an appointment. The monster made his pitch – he was after something mutually beneficial, promising to deliver something the Mayor had only dreamt about – his truest desire. Seeing through the monster's eyes, I could see the confusion, as well as the piqued interest in the other man.

Not able to hear much more than muffled noise, I couldn't make out the conversation, something about power and maybe an offer of eternal life, like with the hardware store manager. With the monster's eyes, I looked into the Mayor's heart. I suspect the Mayor understood what the monster was really offering, and I, too, saw his true desire. Oddly, as disgusted as I was, the monster was also repulsed. Images flashed through the Mayor's mind, those of unfulfilled yearnings for the children he secretly watched from his office window. Shocked at the unexpected revelation, I never suspected the monster might have such a sudden, violent reaction, too.

All at once, the monster demonstrated extreme speed and strength. In a blink, his hands flashed out, thumbs plunging into the Mayor's eyes, fingers wrapping themselves around the man's head. The monster's hands seemed to elongate, growing larger, as they squeezed, fully wrapping around to entwine the fingers. Through the monster's hands, I could feel the crunching of bones, as the skull and neck compressed in that terrible grip. Thankfully, I couldn't hear the Mayor's muted, gurgling scream. Once released, all that was left of the former Mayer of Willow Switch tottered for a moment and fell in a heap. The part of him that used to be his head, clinging loosely to his shoulders, not much more than a bag of pulped flesh.

As the monster coldly turned away, his mind already fixed on the next step of his plan, I caught just a glimpse of the hardware store manager, Mr. Wendis, scooping up the body for disposal.

The vampyr reflected on the night's events, so far. He was surprised at his own actions. Normally, there was no reason to act so rashly. He'd expected the mayor to be a tainted individual, perhaps already given over to evil, hiding under a white wash of false goodness. The vampyr understood the major sins: greed, pride, lust, gluttony, etc., as well as those elements that allowed him entry into a person's will. He could promise almost anything. A lust for children, however, was not within his power.

He remembered a novel one of his thrall, Abigail, gave him to read a few nights ago. Curious to know what a thrall such as this thought so important, she would risk his wrath, by injecting a work of fiction into his nightly study, he acquiesced to her suggestion. At his challenge, she humbly argued that the way her society worked was based on its moral assumptions and that these beliefs were developed upon many sources, including such works of fiction.

Looking into her mind, he saw it for himself. The vampyr had to admit, he had assumed that ancient the Word of the Hebrew God had to be the basis for knowing right and wrong. But this society's moors, although including some of that text, was not based solely upon it. They tended to muddle their ethics with emotion and selfish egotism. So, this revelation interested him. As far as he had experienced, most in this town, a town that claimed to be predominately Christian, was made up of corruptible innocents. He'd found a few that were one extreme or the other, either good or evil. Did the rest of the world follow this same pattern? Perhaps so, but he would have to think about that later.

Not well written, the novel given to him by his thrall did strike a chord, as it strove to tell a story about a character much like himself. This person of ancient royalty spent his time seducing young women and drinking blood. When he imagined pickings might be better elsewhere, he moved, only to get caught and killed. The vampyr thought this book to be a foolish parody if intended to be about himself.

The author's name, Stoker, did not seem familiar. But perhaps this was a descendant of someone that knew him from before? The name reminded him of an old word for a person that removed tree stumps. Did he recall that he knew anyone in this profession? The visions and memories of his past still escaped him, but not completely and not for long.

In the pages of this laughable tail, the villain had thrown a babe to his thrall, for their enjoyment, as well as to nourish them. The vampyr smiled at this ridiculous act, knowing well that such extreme innocents as children would have the most foul, disgusting taste! Even thrall would not partake of them. As bitter and bilious as the taste of evil could be, it could be taken in small amounts. But the sickly-sweet, syrupy taste of a complete innocent, even in the smallest quantities, absolutely nauseated him.

To have assisted this town's mayor, then, even in his lust, rather than gluttony of the young, similarly turned the vampyr's stomach. And that sort of small-mindedness angered him greatly, as well. Although surprised at his own actions, he regretted nothing. If one degenerated or consumed the young, they would be good for nothing but food for his underlings – the vampyr certainly wouldn't touch them! And that would not serve his purpose. Besides, who would grow up to serve him? It simply made no sense and obviously could not be tolerated.

Later that same night, the monster visited the Mayor's assistant. Bitter at the curveballs life had thrown her, she looked as if her 50th birthday was somewhere far behind her when it was actually approaching. Like her apartment, she projected frugality and efficiency, rather than poise and comfort. Again, the monster grinned, chuckling to himself at the sight of her welcome mat, as he knocked, then pushed his way inside. The locks that held the door snapped out of their moorings and flew across the room.

Having just finished her preparations for bed, including her nightly glass of wine, she startled at his forceful knock. She opened her bedroom door cautiously, scowling at the late intrusion. But her mouth dropped open, her face turning white at the sight of him, as she recoiled in fear.

The monster said something. She boldly protested his intrusion, shaking with panic, trying not to pee herself. He crossed the floor smoothly, cornering her, continuing to speak to her. Her expression changed to confusion, then disbelief. As the monster spoke, he stepped closer. He knew how this would end. This was no innocent cowering before him. She would not be as sweet as the librarian, but she would be very useful, nonetheless.

And I knew what that meant. He would find her weakness and corrupt another victim. She would come to him willingly, and he would feed on her. He would savor the delightful vintage of another corrupted soul. And I knew I would wake, sweating and feverish, wanting to throw up in revulsion.

CHAPTER 13

"Thank you for coming in today, Lieutenant. If you don't mind my bluntness, I have to tell you that our talks don't seem to be bearing much fruit, do they?" she asked, moving from behind her desk. "I don't think you are opening up the way you really should. There's very little I can do for you if you aren't willing to discuss your feelings with me, you know." *Besides, I still don't know what to do. No matter where I've looked, or who I've spoken to, I can't explain why you're having these dreams. It's a completely unique condition – no precedence for it found anywhere!* "Besides, you seem to be adapting quite well to them, functionally. Your journal entries are still quite disturbing, but your work is no longer being affected.

"Yes. Um. Thank you, Captain."

"So, I'd like to start today's session a bit differently. In your first few journal entries, you mentioned your sister. I'd like you to tell me about her. Feel free to tell me anything, begin anywhere you like."

"Emily? Well, she and I moved in with our Grammy after our parents died. She was a straight-A student, made honor roll, wanted to be a doctor, stuff like that. She was the perfect kid every parent wants."

Lou paused, to make sure Dr. Spacer wanted her to go on. "Well, Grammy lived off her late husband's pension. By herself, she did okay, but add in two teenage girls and things get tight. Then, shortly after Emily and I moved in, Grammy got sick and Emily spent all of her free time taking care of her.

"I remember asking her once about one of the dances at school. I thought she was just blowing me off. Made me really mad, too. Turns out, like most other girls, she wanted to go, too. Later, I found out she was asked out by three different guys. Three! Well, I just couldn't do life like that. High school was bad enough, just trying to stay out of everyone's way. Which is how I got into the Air Force."

"So, you left for the service right after high school? Hmmm..." For the next half hour or more, Lou told the story and answered questions like, How was high school? Why did you choose to dress the way you did and hang out with the Goth kids? When did you discover you had an aptitude for computer programming? What happened to Emily and your grandmother after you left? Through it all, she avoided telling her doctor the real problem, knowing it would open up a can of worms she'd rather not have to deal with right now. Luvenia Drukner didn't tell Dr. Spacer how she'd betrayed Emily by enlisting. Didn't tell her it was supposed to be her turn to take care of Grammy, while Emily went to Med-school. In retrospect, she would only have had to take care of her grandmother for a short while, as Grammy passed away about a year after Lou left for the Air Force. Louvenia didn't mention this, because she didn't want to admit she owed her sister a debt she could never repay.

*   *   *   *   *   *

Before the timer went off, signaling the end of their session, Spacer said, "I know how difficult it's been lately, for you to make these appointments." Dr. Spacer seemed a bit stiffer than usual, as if unsure how to deliver her information. In the last few weeks, after numerous calls to colleagues for help, Dr. Spacer had finally conceded defeat. This case baffled everyone she spoke to, and she thought it might start making her look bad. "It is for this and other reasons, I have decided to end our mandatory, regularly scheduled meetings. As your journaling seems to be helping, I feel changing our appointments to an as-needed basis may be best. I have already spoken to your commanding officer," Dr. Spacer said with all the authority and seriousness she could muster, trying her best to hide the fact that she had absolutely no idea how to help Lt. Drukner. "You will still submit copies of your journal to me at the end of each week, of course. But as we move forward...."

Maybe Major Westbank had something to do with this? "Really? Um... okay. Sure."

Embarrassed, Dr. Spacer reiterated unnecessarily, "So, just to be clear, what I would like you to do, going forward, is to keep up the journaling. I want to see your entries regularly, just as before. But for the appointments themselves, we'll keep that flexible." Dr. Spacer sat down again, in the big office chair behind her desk. *This meeting just doesn't seem to be going very well,* Spacer thought. "If you feel the need to speak to me, call right away. I'll prioritize your request and make time as soon as I can. How does that sound?"

Sounds like you want to get rid of me, about as much as I'd like to get rid of you. "It sounds like you're really going out of your way for me. Thank you." A moment later, Lou said, "I'll definitely keep up the journaling. You know, I didn't like it much at first, but I think it really helped. I kind of like it now." *Only a few minutes left, and we didn't talk about the dreams at all. Maybe I'm going to get out of here without...*

"Good. Good. So, since we do have a little time left for this session, I would like to know more about a few things," she gestured to the plush couch that her patients used. "Tell me more about this monster. You say he does things your subconscious mind would never imagine." Settling herself back into her familiar groove, she waited a few seconds for effect, before asking, "How does that make you feel?"

Entry 13:
The next several nights ran together, as the monster held court, interviewing those brought before him. The dreams that week became a steady flow of uncomfortable tedium.

The monster's minions brought him people from all over town, a few each night. Judging by the hour and their clothing, I suspected these were night workers and people that kept late hours, such as security guards and transients. But there were others, too: those that had stopped off for a few beers, been out on a date, or were homeless. Forced to stand before the monster, his cunning mind and ability to see into a person's soul judged them. And I learned more about this monster and his ways.

He enjoyed corrupting the innocents, making them into thrall. Very much like the vampires in the movies, they would have to feed on fresh blood and avoid the sunlight. Those that were not innocent, that were already somewhat corrupted individuals, like the hardware store guy, he chose to make minions. Minions would be able to work without rest, had no fear of sunlight, but craved dead flesh to survive.

As terrible as that might sound, however, the third choice proved to be the most difficult to stomach. Those of little use to him or those that refused to be corrupted, as well as those that were far too depraved, became a source of fresh blood for his thrall, then food for his minions. Those victims cried, kicked, and screamed in terror, as he announced his verdict over them. I could see their eyes fill with fear beyond tears, as the horror of their fate dawned.

Although only a few people were brought to him each night, I got the impression he could quietly work his way through the entire town, if that was what he wanted to do.

Like Abigail, Penelope dreamed as she transformed. She dreamed of her life in all its bitterness and disappointment, for this was what had corrupted her. Told at an early age that she could do anything, Penelope always strove for greatness. Top 3 percent of her class? Not good enough. Fast track in the management program, and up the corporate ladder? Not good enough. Better companies and higher wages? Not good enough. Married to one of the nicest, most loving, and supportive of men? Not good enough.

That she'd always pushed herself so hard shouldn't have been a bad thing. But it created in her a disappointment in everything around her, as well as everything she'd earned. She found she couldn't respect anyone that hadn't achieved the levels she had. But anyone above her was competition, meaning she couldn't respect them either.

And where had all of these burned bridges led her? She was the Mayor's Assistant in a podunk little town, in one of the poorest areas in all of the United States. And she hated being someone else's lacky. She hated His Honor the Mayor, she hated her job, she hated this town and all its simple people living simple little lives, and most of all, she hated herself.

*   *   *   *   *   *

Miss Penelope Bishop, the former assistant to the late Mayor Kent Kingsly, woke up in her bed, just like she did every morning. But something was different. First of all, the clock told her she'd slept away the entire day. She also couldn't see a thing in the pitch-black room. *No. Wait. Yes, I can see. Why can I make out the room, when I know it's dark out? And why is it dark out?* The oddness followed her into the bathroom, where she decided not to turn on the light. Now that she concentrated, she could see just fine.

It came to her and she remembered and knew that the events of the night before really had happened. She'd been visited by her new employer. *No, that's not right. Not employer. Boss? Yes...no. Master. Yes. Master,* she thought. A warm feeling went through her then - being owned, body and soul. She somehow felt comforted by the thought.

Once he'd gone, she'd been in a liquid and languid haze, feeling nothing, but peace. The Master's minions, led by Dwight, whom she recognized from the hardware store, had come into her apartment and quietly made it secure against sunlight. Just to check that she hadn't been dreaming, Penelope walked around her apartment, window to window, smiling as she inspected their work. Panels had been placed over each window, in such a way that they looked normal from the outside, but blocked out all incoming light.

Now that she was awake, she realized how hungry she'd become, so she took a quick look in her refrigerator. All of the healthy food she normally kept on hand was still there: juice, greens, vegetables, milk. But nothing appealed to her. In fact, everything she looked at turned her stomach in revulsion. Like a wild animal, she wasn't just hungry, she craved. *Maybe I can find what I want at the grocery,* she told herself as she threw on a blouse and a pair of jeans.

She left without checking herself in the mirror, as she normally did. There just didn't seem to be any need. She felt good. No, not just good, she felt sleek and sensual, healthy and vibrant.

She paused, however, noticing the reflection in her car's rear view. Ignoring the fact that she was partially see-through, she marveled at the image it showed her. If the mirror wasn't lying, her wrinkles and greying hair were gone, replaced with youthful skin and rich, flowing hair. *I'm...beautiful. And I'm young. But, even when I was young, I was never this...gorgeous!* She looked down at herself, feeling the firm breasts and gentle muscle tone beneath her clothing.

With a hungry, lecherous smile, she started up the old Toyota, realizing the local market wouldn't have what she needed. *But Joe's Steakhouse might. Yes. Joe's might have just what I need,* she thought. And she was starving!

*   *   *   *   *   *

Starting to worry about Jimmy-Wayne, Linsey Mae's tip-game was off. She'd lost the spring in her step, and her wide-smiling, baby-doll attitude had slipped more times than she could count, her thoughts bouncing back and forth from sadness to anger and back. *It's been more than a week! He's never taken off this long.* Smiling now, as memories popped into her head. *He always comes back, bringing me flowers, acting all bashful and such. He says he's sorry, with them big ole puppy dog eyes that just melt the big ole mad-on I got. Then I pout a bit, and he grabs me up and takes me back to his place.* Then, frowning, *Maybe this time, he's gone for good,* she worried. Then, turning angry, *It's that floozy with the big hooters! I bet she's the one that's got him all wrapped around her little finger.* Turning sad again, she thought, *Maybe something's happened to him! I should tell the Sheriff.* Now angry, *No. He's just trying to get back at me. That jerk!*

Just then, she noticed a repeat of the events of last week, when Jimmy-Wayne disappeared. Only this time, it was a different woman making all the heads turn. Dressed in a decent blouse and jeans, she didn't seem like the type that would attract so much attention – especially compared to the cut-off shorty-shorts, push-up bra, and skimpy, knotted tank top that Linsey Mae wore as her uniform.

The difference was, this one didn't stay long before leaving with someone. That someone wasn't her Jimmy-Wayne, of course. But the similarity was just too much. Linsey Mae ran into the back room, feeling herself tearing up. She'd put her mascara on too thick, to ruin it with a good cry!

*   *   *   *   *   *

"My truck's just over here, Maam."

"Maam? You're so cute," Penelope purred, holding onto Franklin's strong, young arm. "I just wanted to get out of there and look at the stars with you. Do you know somewhere we could go that has a good view of the stars?"

"Uh, yes, Maam," Franklin said sheepishly, realizing he just called her "Maam" again, but unable to keep himself from doing it. "Y-yes, Miss Penelope. I shore do," flushing even more. *How lucky am I, right? First job out of High School, first pay-check, first time out with the guys, and I catch the eye of the hottest thing I ever did see! Look at the stars? Right. She's gonna let me... we're gonna...oh-oh-oh boy!*

As they drove past the highway and headed out of town, her desire growing hotter, she decided they'd gone far enough. *Poor little Frankie,* she thought sarcastically. *So young. So full of vitality! Look how the life energy just pulses around him. I can hear his blood pulsing, rushing through him, his heartbeat elevated with the excitement of the event to come, rising each time I casually touch his knee or stroke his arm. He's going to taste GOOD.* The only thing that had been holding her back was the possibility of flipping the truck over into the ditch next to the road, but she was hungry. She didn't care about anything else. And she wanted to take her prize now!

CHAPTER 14

Entry 14:
Last night turned out to be a bit different, and scary in an entirely different way. Last night, the monster met with the town's leaders.

I saw through the monster's eyes, as he entered the courthouse meeting room with his small entourage of minions. The Mayor's secretary and another man were there, as well. As they walked in, the men and one older woman turned in their seats, curious about this man and his invitation. They wondered, too, at the absence of the Mayor who had invited them.

The monster waited until he had positioned himself near the podium. He paused for effect, scanning the faces in the room, as they waited for the Mayor's mysterious colleague to pitch them the promised deal. He looked into each curious, but doubtful face, gleaning their desires as he did. A mix of oligarchy and businessmen from all over the county, these eight individuals began to grow impatient. How could anyone make them richer and more powerful than they already were?

Then the monster began to speak. With the help of a local lawyer, he outlined his plans. Intrigued, his audience began asking questions all at once. "Where is the money coming from?" and "What's in it for us?" showing their frustration.

These power-hungry individuals wanted the reward, but not the risk. Their frustration grew. The lone woman got up to leave, but the monster's minions covered each of the exits. At that moment, his thrall came in, positioning themselves, one to each of those gathered. Distracted by the sudden entrance of so many hot women, the voices of dissent stuttered to a halt.

The monster took this opportunity to walk the room. He slowly made his way around, looking each seated man in the eyes. He knew their desires. Now he saw the corruption in their hearts. He spoke to their souls. Silently, one by one, they came to an agreement.

He took his place again at the podium, the room now still and quiet. All attention focused intently on him and his next word or gesture. He paused, enjoying the moment. Then he nodded to his thrall. As one, they moved closer to their appointed victim. Gentle hands and lustful eyes caressed and entrapped. Even the old woman sat mesmerized by the display. With an unexpected movement, the thrall struck. Shock spread on the gathered faces, a few letting out startled half-screams. They looked to the monster, with fear and doubt, but none resisted. The monster held them in his gaze and smiled as his thrall fed.

At that moment, a new term revealed itself to me in the monster's mind: the tasted. Different than minions or thrall, who had both seen physical changes, the "tasted" would not be changed. They would only receive a new addiction. They would carry out their normal lives, but they would do all they were asked, yearning to be tasted again. No other addiction could rule them. And they would stay enslaved to him until the monster released them. These leaders' every dime and every moment now hinged on the monster's leadership.

"That is enough, dear thrall. These are not to be fed from completely, only tasted. And in doing this, unlike the others you bring me, you will be able to drink from them regularly. As long as they continue to serve me, that is." The thrall obediently, but reluctantly stopped feeding to lick the neck wounds closed and clean themselves of every succulent drop.

Yes, the thrall are very useful in their own way, however limited. The Vampyr thought to himself. *I wish I could have nothing but minions, as they can carry out my orders, even in daylight. Unfortunately, they just don't last very long, having to eat older and older dead flesh, in order to retain their vigor, eventually rotting away completely. Although less durable, the thrall are still useful. And they do have a particular penchant for locating the sweet corruptible.* The Vampyr thought hungrily.

> But what was it? In these dreams, I can only see
> what the monster sees. So, I could only make out
> that the monster's project involved a large building,
> as part of a massive construction project near the
> center of town. But parts of the project also ran
> through the town. Extra roads? A pipeline, maybe?
> I couldn't tell.

"Good morning, Master Sergeant," Lou said, returning his salute. She entered and took the cup of the Corporal's coffee he offered, allowing herself a moment to smell the aroma, before taking a sip. This was the first time she'd seen his office. Always before, he'd met her at the front desk and walked her back to the range.

Politely, he waived her over to one of the two leather-bound chairs situated in front of his desk. Unlike Captain Spacer's office, and except for the two chairs, this one looked more like an office, where actual work might get done: filing cabinets, old-style swivel chair behind a metal desk, plain, white blinds covering a faux window (as were all windows in a complex more than 2000 feet underground).

"Please call me something other than Master Sergeant, at least while we're alone. It's just too stuffy," he chuckled. "Greg is better.

"So, what brings you to see me today? We're not scheduled for a lesson and most people don't just drop by here unannounced. Do you prefer Lieutenant Drukner, or should I call you Luvenia?"

"Call me Lou, if you don't mind." She appreciated his casual demeanor. It seemed more genuine than Dr. Spacer's overly pleasant attitude or Major Westbank's uncomfortable stiffness. Although just as crisp and serious as any other, TwoDogs seemed to wear his uniform like he was born in it, which told her a lot about him. For one, he was not just another stuffed shirt. She could easily imagine him looking just as formal in a Hawaiian shirt, throwing a Frisbee around in a dog park. "Well, Greg, how do I start? I guess you could say that I've been having some interesting dreams, which was the reason for our meeting in Dr.

Spacer's waiting area. Well, the dreams aren't so important, as the fact that they've got me thinking.

"Normally, I would go to a pastor or someone like that. But, although I know they've studied the Bible, sometimes I get the feeling they don't really understand what they're preaching – in a practical sense. So, I wanted to talk to you, instead. I mean, for one thing, you're easier to talk to," she said, trying to hold back a blush. "But, more than that, I get the feeling you have a more realistic understanding of this stuff, that you may be able to…. So, I thought…."

He nodded politely, curious to know where this was going. Though still unsure of herself, she continued, "Well, I know that God is everywhere and all. But I just don't feel like He's very close. Or, rather, that He's where he's always been, but I'm the one that's far away. Does that make any sense?"

TwoDogs leaned in seriously, "Well, tell me this: let's say you died today (just a what if, mind you – I don't really want you to die)," he chuckled. "So, you died and walked up to the pearly gates. And you see Jesus there. And He asks you a question, 'Why should I let you in?' What would your answer be?"

Lou thought hard. Oddly, no one had ever asked her such a question. "I guess I'd have to say that I've tried to be good, having been raised in a Christian home and going to church and all. I remember making the Jesus prayer when I was a kid, and I got baptized at age nine. So…I guess that's… Is that what you meant?"

"So, what are you telling me? You're saved because you're a good person, or you're saved because you gave your life to Jesus?"

Lou could only feel confusion. "I'm not sure. I mean, I know that I'm saved. I just don't…know…"

"Okay. Let's come back to that. You probably know the answer. It's just not coming to you. No problem. So, let's clear up a few things first. You tell me if there is anything wrong with what I say, or if you don't believe I'm right, okay? I can also clarify if there's anything you don't understand.

"First of all, if I gifted you with an expensive gift, when would it be yours? When you received it, right?" Lou nodded, and he went on. "But if I let you pay me for it, or if you did something to earn it, would it still be a gift?"

"No. If I paid for it, it's my property. And if I earned it, it's mine by right."

"Exactly. It's only a gift if I give it freely, and it's only yours if you take it from me." He went on, as she smiled. "Well, Heaven, the eternal happy place, is a gift. It cannot be paid for or earned, only willingly accepted.

"Now let's talk about those of us here on Earth: you, me, your commanding officer, everyone. We're all sinners. Would you agree with that?"

"Sure. We're all born into it. That's what makes this world so flawed, violent, and diseased. It's our in-born disobedience of God, as well as the selfishness that comes to us naturally."

"Right. And, because of this, we cannot save ourselves. If the penalty for sin is death, we would have to die to pay the debt. So, if we die to pay the debt, how can we live to receive any sort of reward? Also, God created us to be with Him, and He still wants us with Him. But God is Holy and cannot accept anything tainted with sin."

"Okay. Wait. That makes no sense," Luvenia began, "How can we get into Heaven if we're condemned to death because of our sin? And, as much as He wants us, we can't come to Him anyway, because He can't stand the sin we were born with," she said, feeling like a little girl back in Sunday School.

"Exactly! Now, remember that God is also merciful, so He provided a way for us to get around all of that."

"Jesus!" she said, snapping her fingers. "He sent His son to pay for our sins, so that we wouldn't have to, AND so that we could come to him freely, by choice."

"Very good. See? You remember more than you thought. Jesus not only died, so that we wouldn't have to, but His death also removed our sin. And we know this because Jesus didn't just die in our place, He conquered death and came back from the dead. No one has ever been able to do that – ever!

The Sergeant's eyebrows rose expectantly, reminding Lou of a professor she once had, "So how do we know we are saved?"

"Well, by faith, obviously." Then she thought again and added, "but not temporary faith or head-knowledge. It's got to be a heart thing – like the trust we had as kids when we knew our parents would always be there for us."

"There you have it. If that's what you believe, and you've made a heart-level commitment, you're saved. And nothing on this Earth can take that from you. Of all the things we are given or experience, salvation is the one thing that can never be taken from us.

"You still look a bit confused. It's pretty simple, but you may want to take a while to think about it. Let's meet back up later, and we can talk some more when you're ready."

Entry 15:
It's been a few days since my last entry. Duty's been keeping me extra busy lately. But most of my dreams have been pretty bland. Well, not exactly. Just more of the monster holding court, passing sentence on several more citizens, and feeding. Disgusting! But otherwise, somewhat boring.

Except for one particular incident. Apparently, the town's rumor mill caused the local preacher to start sticking his nose into things. He was brought before the monster one night, looking like he'd been pulled out of bed. I couldn't tell, at first, if they argued, exactly. But the monster raged fiercely at the preacher, and the preacher held something to his chest for dear life, occasionally throwing back defensive words.

We have not met, sir. But I do know you by reputation" Taken abruptly from his study, while preparing this Sunday's message, Paul Everett Murphy, Pastor of the Willow Switch Community Bible Church, quaked as he was taken before this stranger. The men that took him were known to him but acted strangely, vastly different than anything he'd seen before – almost as if they weren't the same people. *And their breath! Good Lord, what the devil have they been eating?* He relaxed a little at the compliment but still found it difficult not to tremble.

"You are the leader of this community, are you not?" The stranger's eyes sparkled with intelligence and quiet power and seemed to penetrate into his brain. The minister nodded. "You take responsibility for the spiritual development of this town?" After the preacher nodded again, the stranger's eyes flared with sudden anger. "So, you are the one that is to blame."

"I- I don't under- understand," Murphy managed. Then, beginning to fill with indignance, "Why have I been brought here? Who are you? What do you want with me? So what if you know who I am? A lot of people know me. That doesn't give you any right to..."

"You lead your flock in lies, sir!" the stranger roared. "You tell them what they want to hear, and you make them feel," finding the word, he spit it out with disdain, "spiritual."

"As for my name, it is not as important as your fate. As for rights, what right do you have to tell your parishioners they must be good little boys and girls, adhering to all the rules and traditions, in order to be saved? What right have you to tell them that their faith must not be strong enough because they do not possess all that they desire? Then you threaten them with hellfire and damnation to keep them in line, as you freely preach your own opinions."

At this outburst, the ones that held him stepped back into the shadows, emboldening their captive. "You can't say that. I preach the good book! It's sacred," he answered, throwing out his chest and standing tall.

"Yes. The book you clutch to yourself so valiantly is indeed sacred," the stranger said gently. "But you only use it as a reference, a required ingredient in the formula. But when you deliver your messages, those messages are yours alone. They are not His," he said, pointing up, "You push your own agenda, not His. I find it amusing, that you should describe it as sacred when you use it as anyone might a common dictionary or encyclopedia. Do you not realize? The book you hold in your hand is not a collection of authors, parroting a common theme. It is the actual and living Word of God!"

> The preacher was clearly losing the battle, looking very uncomfortable by the monster's accusations. As with every previous dream, I could only hear muffled sounds. Most everything was visual. But the argument seemed pretty clear. The monster was accusing the preacher of something. Something that convicted him and put him on the defensive. And the preacher was losing.

"Of course, its the word of God-"

"NO!" the stranger shouted, stepping towards the tall, wiry, minister, causing him to stumble backward in fear. He tripped, just as the strange man, so tall and menacing, suddenly reached out, snatching the book from Pastor Murphy's hands, causing him to fall back against the wall.

> At one point, the monster snatched the object out of the preacher's hands. It was a book. Red-hot fire shot through the monster's hand, and I felt the pain, like holding tightly to molten metal! The pain was so intense, I couldn't even cry out. But the monster ignored it, shaking the book at the object of his wrath. It couldn't be just any book. This had to be a Bible, now obviously significant to the accusations against the skinny preacher.

"You are so pathetic," the stranger sneered. "Just like the rest of mankind. God speaks, the chosen record it, and the masses whine that there is no 'proof' that God exists. And it is so very simple. All anyone needs to do is read it. In all its hundreds of pages, it delivers but one message: God created you to be with Him. And even though you reject Him, still He offers you a simple way to come to Him."

"Well, yes. I mean, of course. I-"

"Simpleton! How much clearer must it be made, before you understand? The words in this volume are actual words God has spoken and is even now speaking. If you do not understand this, you are as deaf as you are stupid. Your own God, the one you profess to follow. He SPEAKS to you. Here. In this book!"

The monster paused, calming himself. "If only you would have used this book to prepare them, I would be powerless here. But instead, you reveled in the power it gave you over them," he paused. Then suddenly enraged, "As your sheep go happily to the slaughter!"

Finally, the monster's tirade concluded in a sudden burst of furious energy. He threw the now smoking book into the preacher's chest. The man went down, more than just the breath taken out of him, as he openly wept and clutched the smoking Bible once again to his chest.

The searing pain in my hand was replaced by an alternating numbness and a pain almost as bad as when holding the Bible. Having experienced a 3rd-degree burn as a kid, I understood what was happening. I managed to catch a glimpse, as the monster glanced down at his hand. The flesh, almost completely missing from his palm and fingers, looked more like melted wax, than any burn I'd ever seen. White bone and seared tendons shone out from the damage.

Even now, the monster didn't flinch, his pain tolerance superhuman. It flashed through the monster's mind that the missing flesh was only a nuisance, as it would regrow the next time he fed.

The minions led the preacher away, completely broken by the accusations. He looked up, into the monster's eyes, shock and disbelief turning to an agreement, as he conceded. Whatever the monster had accused him of, the monster was right.

CHAPTER 15

Entry 14:
Compared to my last entry, this one is probably pretty mundane. But I have to record this, as I think it might be significant. I heard something the other day, that you can't read in your dreams. But I remember reading a few things in mine, such as the name of the town. Of course, you may chalk this up to the dreamer trying to fill in details. Well, it gets better. Last night, I realized I've been reading complete and coherent passages, whole articles in fact. This further convinces me these aren't normal dreams.

The monster has been catching up on recent history, through magazines and periodicals each night. And I've been waking up each morning, knowing more about current events than most of my peers!

In the local paper, The Willowswitch Gazette, three stories caught my attention. First, news of a fire that had burned down the newly built Tuminov place, a recently built mansion out on the old Perkins Ranch property. Another small article mentioned the local hardware store's big "Welcome" mat giveaway, involving every residence in town. But the article that really caught my eye had to do with the groundbreaking ceremony for a new clinic, the largest and most progressive project to come to Willow Switch since the railroad came through.

My first dream involved a house fire, the monster's relationship with the hardware store manager, and the fact that he smiled every time he saw a "Welcome" mat. And now mention of a new project in town.

These coincidences led me to do some research on the little town of Willow Switch. I couldn't find anything at first but decided to seek out some of the publications the monster was reading. I could at least compare the memories of my dreams with what I found. And BINGO! So, I've made an appointment to take them to Dr. Spacer later this week, to prove I'm not just dreaming, that this is somehow a reflection of reality, not my over-active imagination or subconscious.

Side Note: I also looked up vampires on the web. What I found was mostly book references and fan-fiction. But all of the articles and websites noted pretty much the same basic things:
  • sensitive to silver, garlic, and crosses

- can't walk on holy ground
- killed by a wooden stake through the heart or by sunlight
- can't enter a home unless invited

There were other things, too, but not everyone mentioned or agreed on them. Some were fairly obscure:

- cut off their head to kill them
- must be buried at a crossroads
- weakness to fire, white oak, rosewood, and wormwood
- casts no reflection
- can't be recorded on audio or video

Apparently, they are also incredibly OCD, too. If they encounter a knot, they have to untie it. If grain is spilled, they are compelled to count the kernels. Weird stuff like that. But they all agreed a vampire is super-quick, super-strong, and very intelligent.

*On a different subject, I just have to write down something I've been thinking about a lot lately. I met with Greg again. I was feeling really disjointed about my life. Even without the stress of these dreams and the strange, terrifying things I'm seeing, I'm still confused about some things.

I told him that I feel myself as being far away from God. Our conversation was interesting.

Even though he didn't really seem to address my question, he talked about why I think I'm saved.

After seeing the monster with the town preacher, although I couldn't hear anything, I'm thinking: What could their argument have been about? What would concern the monster so much, that he would take the time to accuse the minister of something – something that made him angry enough to ignore burning the flesh from his own hand? I have to think it was something the guy did or was doing – or maybe didn't do that he should have done, right?

More than any other reason, I think this may have had something to do with how the preacher did his job. Could the townsfolk have been better prepared against the monster? Because, if so, what kind of preparation would that be? How could a person defend himself against someone looking inside them for a flaw, in order to corrupt them into evil? Was it possible?

Thinking back, I suppose I have seen a few that weren't corruptible. (They were made into food!) But what was it that allowed them to resist? How had they been strong enough when most others weren't? Would I be strong enough to resist, too?

*   *   *   *   *   *

Head bowed over his Bible and notes, Gregory prayed. As usual, he talked to God about his study, prayed blessings for his family and co-workers, and prayed protection for his country, its leadership, and those that served in the armed forces. Most of all, he prayed for the strength to get over his own issues so that he could see his family again and maybe start leading a regular life.

My dad and I always fought. It seemed I was always such a disappointment to him. When I left, I had no idea facing him again would be so difficult. I imagined I would have the medals, rank, and reputation that would force him to see the error in his logic, earn his respect, and embrace me as his son. But how much would be enough? That's the fear. Not to mention the injuries from the crash. I want to go home, and I want to get this over with. But it's been so long already. How can I face my dad? How can I face the rest of my family? Lord, please help me find the answer. I just don't know on my own.

Just as he was ending his prayer, remembering to give thanks for his new friend, Lt. Drukner, he heard the sound of footsteps from down the hall. Guessing his visitor was not one of his own people, he straightened and opened his eyes.

She knew she didn't have to, but she couldn't help knocking. It was the polite thing to do. "Do you have a few minutes to talk?"

"Sure," Master Sergeant Gregory TwoDogs said, sticking the papers he was working on into his Bible and setting it aside. "Just taking some notes as I study. It's nice to see you again."

Between shooting lessons and my visits for coffee, we see each other almost every day. But he's actually happy to see me. She thought, beginning to feel warm inside. But then her worries intruded again, causing her to shove those thoughts aside and get back to the reason for her visit.

"It's just that I had a few questions about what we talked about before – about God and stuff." His wide smile became more serious, and she sat down at his gesture. "I understand what you said about heaven and salvation, and I agree – that was a very succinct way of putting it. My problem is: What about here on Earth? I made a decision for salvation when I was a kid. But then I didn't have time to do much more than go to church once in a while. How was I supposed to become some sort of "Super-Christian," like the Bible tells me I should?"

"Let me ask you this: Why is the central message of the Bible that of salvation? Because He wants us to wear His team colors and sit in the stands, or because He wants us to be with Him?"

Lou stared at the seams on the sergeant's uniform as she replied, "I don't know. Be with Him I guess."

"Exactly. Now, what do you know about His nature?" Pausing to give her time to begin thinking, he went on, "Besides being all-powerful, all-knowing, and everywhere, He's Holy, right? Which is why He can't stand sin. He wants us, warts and all, no matter what terrible things we've done, and He's willing to forgive any sin we bring Him in repentance.

"Sure, heaven is the ultimate gift, but in the meantime, He wants us to walk with Him. God is not about the behavior, as much as He's about the relationship. You've seen people that act like Christians, but you get the feeling they might be faking it? That's because they aren't walking with Him. That's why He wants us to have a relationship with Him – you can't fake it if you really are walking with Him.

"That relationship is like that of a parent, but a perfect parent – no abuse, no neglect, no dysfunction, no abandonment. And, as the perfect parent, He wants the best for us. Now, I don't know what kind of home life you had, but good parents love their children, no matter their flaws, right? Did your mother disown you for repeatedly stealing cookies from the jar? No. But neither did she leave them within easy reach, after punishing you. She put them on a higher shelf, to make it easier for you to obey. Right?

"Well, our temptation to sin is similar, and some sins are more difficult to resist for some than for others. Some have a weakness for stealing cookies. Some have a weakness for climbing on counters to get to those cookies. Our society has argued for blaming these flaws on nature or nurture, as a way to justify themselves and excuse them from the fact that it is the individual's responsibility, to alter their own behavior. But a good father loves his children so much, that he can't let the kids stay flawed by their sinful tendencies.

"This is why the Christian life is about the walk – the relationship – living life more abundantly with Him. After salvation, He sends us the Holy Spirit, to guide us into a richer relationship."

After a bit of thought, Lou asked, "But how do you know you're doing it right?"

"I've heard these kinds of questions before. You're looking for a gauge, like a dipstick, to find out how good you are. Look around any church. You'll find people giving their time, their money, and their energy. They all look like good, mature Christians, but only some of them really are. That's because the only way to gauge spiritual maturity is by a person's true character, not outer trappings. The fact that you're concerned about your own spiritual maturity, is actually a good sign.

"So, I'll give you my personal prescription: Find the time to read the Bible each day. Read it prayerfully, constantly asking for guidance, for God to reveal Himself to you in it. Pray on it, read it, and take notes on your study – even just 5 minutes a day. Think on it throughout the day, and let the Holy Spirit guide you.

"Commit to this for at least a month, and journal your thoughts and feelings as you go. I guarantee you'll see a difference. It may only be a small change, but you'll see it."

"Journal it, eh? Now you sound like Captain Spacer," she laughed, realizing she'd just undone all the ridicule she'd made of Spacer's advice to journal. *Maybe journaling wasn't such a lame idea after all.*

* * * * * *

"I sure am sorry, Doreen. I just feel terrible. Sharon and I tried our best. You know we did. You two really broke up?" Deputy Reed said gently, as he played with the telephone cord, his booted feet up on the desk. *It's all my fault. I should have been the one to talk to Sheriff Lange, not Sharon. Maybe he'd have listened to me. Doreen's too good a woman to treat her like he was doing.*

"That's okay, Tommy. Don't worry your head about it. How's the office running, now he's spendin' more time there?" Doreen tried to put up a good front, but inside, her heart was breaking. A woman of her age just didn't have too many decent prospects left.

"Oh, sure. He's here a lot more. But so are the other guys he's deputized. Some of 'em I've never seen before. They's all out patrollin' all the time, but never callin' dispatch. They report directly to Lange. He swears they're doin' a great job, but they don't bring nobody in. Jail's empty." Deputy Reed sighed, taking his feet off the desk. Even if there wasn't anything to do, if Sheriff Lange caught him looking relaxed, he'd hit the roof.

"I don't understand it. Buddy O'Dell and me, we always kept it under control, just us by ourselves. But reported crimes and other emergencies really are down, lately. In fact, nights have kind of become like a ghost town or somethin'. I mean, what's everybody doin', if they ain't getting' into trouble once in a while?

"Which is why I've been the one returning the Sheriff's library books, picking up his dry cleaning, getting his lunch for him, and all sorts of stuff. He won't even let me investigate last night's break-in over at the morgue!

"I tell you, Doreen. I used to be a Sheriff's Deputy. Now I'm just some kind of gopher. Go fer this, go fer that. Not that I got nothin' else to do. But, dang-it, Doreen!" he stopped himself, forcing himself to whisper, "This ain't what I signed on for!"

Entry 17:
Just got back from Dr Spacer's office. She said these publications don't really prove anything, as I could have read them and forgotten. Which is totally ridiculous!

Except, like she pointed out, I couldn't possibly be dreaming of a real vampire, who reads minds and can turn onto mist.

So, maybe she's right. I don't know. I think I'm more confused now than I was before. Just when I think I'm sure, doubts creep in, and I start thinking maybe it really is just all my imagination. But it can't be! URGH!!

Good news, though: with the latest phase of Pinpoint's testing done, she managed to get me a 3-day pass, so I can go check it out myself, maybe put my mind at ease. I don't leave for a few days, so I'll have time to locate the town and plan my trip. Then I'll find out if I'm crazy, or if there really is such a thing as monsters.

Greg said it might feel like taking medicine now, but that it would eventually seem more like taking vitamins. Pulling out her Bible again, Lou sighed. *This is the hardest part of my new commitment. It's not so much the reading, as it's the remembering to read! REALLY not convenient.* Sighing again, she opened it up to where she left off the day before. *Gotta keep at it, though – make it a habit.*

Lou had cried just a little when she'd unwrapped the still new copy her sister had given her years ago. Taking TwoDogs' advice, she read a few verses each day, whatever seemed like a complete thought, and made a note in a fresh journal she bought just for her Bible notes. *Call me Lieutenant Journal-Girl!* She giggled to herself. *My old English teacher would roll over in his grave if he saw how much I write nowadays... especially if he knew I think I might actually like it!*

After a short, but heart-felt prayer, Luvenia felt as if she'd just put on a warm coat against a winter chill. She felt good. She noticed that a kind of peace followed her throughout her day. And even when she felt stressed now, she knew a certain kernel of joy at her core. *All this time, I was feeling so far from God. Now, I feel His hand on me, almost like I'm standing right next to Him.*

CHAPTER 16

Entry 18:
I decided to keep up the journaling during my trip.
I'm kind of getting into it, and it really is rather...
satisfying? (I hate to say "therapeutic," but it really
is, I guess.)

Oh! And I found the town of Willow Switch. I looked
up the article on the clinic that the monster is
building. It's just off one of the highways that pass
through the toolies, out in Arkansas, of all places!
Luckily, it's a single Greyhound ride away from
Little Rock AFB.

Also, I read up on the medical facility the monster
is building. Looks like it's a Hematology research
facility, researching cures for blood diseases. Go
figure, right? A vampire that wants to cure blood
disease! Quite a step up from the obvious blood
bank idea, though. This guy's thinking big.

BTW, packing sucks! I thought I'd go light: one change
of clothes and an extra pair of undies, in a carry-on
bag. But I keep thinking of more stuff I think I'll need.
I think I've re-packed at least 5 times already!

Entry 19:
Wow! Nothing like a long, uncomfortable flight in the jump seat of a cargo plane, followed by another hour or more in a cramped, smelly bus with no leg room! Now I remember why I accumulated all that leave: I hate traveling! It's so much stress, rarely comfortable (no matter what the TV ads say), and it always takes too long.

Testing of Pinpoint's satellite targeting system, now that we're out of the simulacrum phase, came just at the right time. And, since test data is going to take a while to process, Dr. Spacer was able to get Major Westbank to authorize this pass. And I won't be needed back until after they're done! WooHoo!

My muscles are stiff, my back is sore, and my head hurts. So much for my first day in Willow Switch. I found the only thing that passed for a hotel, so I think I'm just going to take some aspirin and crash, instead of looking around tonight.

*   *   *   *   *   *

"How was the French toast, Honey?" the matronly, older woman, dressed in a faded pink uniform, with a big "Libby's Diner" name tag on, asked with a wide smile. As small as this place was, Lou assumed this slightly pudgy woman was probably Libby. At such an early hour, the place should have been busier, but Lou seemed to have the place all to herself.

"Mmf! Heavenly!" Lou said, swallowing down the last morsel and shyly wiping a drip of butter from her mouth.

"Well, I gotta tell ya. My little Dougie, he's the fella back in the kitchen, he used to like 'em just the way you do: no syrup, extra butter, and lots of powdered sugar." She leaned in close and whispered, "Watchin' his weight, now. But he used to put 'em away, back in the day. Let me tell you." Lou smiled, as Libby giggled like she'd just given away her family's most humorous secret.

As Libby reached for the plate, Lou tried to be subtle, "Such a nice little town. It must be so nice to live here. Um, so, what's new? I mean, to an outsider, it kind of looks like I've stepped back in time," she blushed with embarrassment. "What I mean to say is: Is there anything, um, different, or, um, anything... going on lately?" It took all the control she could muster, to maintain her positive demeanor, but she felt like slinking under the table and out the door.

"Why, nothin' here ever changes much, Sweetie. We got ol' Bobby-Ray come to set up his tent - that's Reverend Beatty. He comes up around here about once a year or so. Is that what you're lookin' for?" Libby gave Lou her best smile. "Me and Dougie always like goin' to his revival. He's real spiritual. We never miss it. Dougie always insists on takin' me every year. He's such a good boy."

Disappointed at her first foray into detective work, Luvenia lied, telling Libby that sounded interesting, and left a generous tip before leaving. If she hadn't been so wrapped up in her self-analysis, she might have caught Libby's frightened look.

Back in the kitchen, Dougie put down the half-chewed leg, wiped his mouth, and called to his mother in the dining area, "What was that about, Ma? That little girl gettin' nosey into our business?" Along with his strength and stamina, his hearing had improved greatly, since joining the new master.

"No, dear," she said quickly. "She's just another clueless tourist – like that Tuminov fella and his wife. She's just afraid of gettin' bored, that's all." Libby didn't know what she was afraid of more, what Dougie might do to the girl, or what he might decide to do to her. And she couldn't help wondering what had come over Dougie lately. Despite her best efforts, he'd always been something of a bully. *Not that any of those mean little children ever took the time to give little Dougie a break. Not his fault he was always twice as big as any other kid his age.* But until recently, he had never been so dominating, almost paranoid, like this before. *And his breath! Ugh!* Whatever it was, though, it scared her too much to even think about.

Satisfied, Dougie picked up the leg again, remembering Old Mister Patterson, a regular at the diner. Patterson would come in every night at about the same time, and order two slices of the diner's famous apple pie and a glass of milk. Then he would read his book for nearly an hour. It was a nightly ritual. As Dougie gnawed another bite, he grimaced at the fattiness of the meat, but wondered at the odd flavor he was picking up that seemed to compensate. Then he had it. The source of the subtle flavor finally dawned on him - sweetened apples and a hint of cinnamon.

*   *   *   *   *   *

The owner of Heyes' Pharmacy let out a sigh, as he let his mind wander. Sweeping an already well-swept front walk, he enjoyed the cool breeze, drifting in from the North. At the hottest hour of the day, it was easier re-sweeping the walk in the shade of the overhang, than doing anything inside, where it wouldn't cool off until later in the afternoon. Keeping himself busy doing anything, was better than appearing lazy, even when business was so slow.

"Warm, slow day." He reflected aloud.

"One of many warm, slow days lately," Charles Murphy affirmed from the porch of the market next door. Like Eddie Heyes, he was re-stacking boxes of detergent on a display he'd set up and stacked there earlier that morning, just to have an excuse to work outside.

"Yep. One of many. That's for sure, Chuck."

Noticing a faint tinkling of chimes or bells, he looked up, closing his eyes against the brightness of the day reflected off the white-painted front of the building across the street. He turned his head to catch the sound more clearly. It seemed to come in on the wind. Looking in that direction, he noticed something in the distance, coming closer.

"Visitor coming. Looks to be a girl," the shopkeeper said.

"She coming this way?"

"We don't get too many new people come through here. You thinkin' it's a tourist or something? Probably some kind of tourist. I expect."

"Tourist? Yeah. More'n likely a tourist. Who'd be comin' to set down roots in Willow Switch?" The grocer's mind went back in time, to the rumors he'd heard before Tuminov moved in.

"I don't reckon it'll be another one o' them movie-type fellers. I know things about that kind o' stuff," Heyes bragged, waggling his thumb at himself. "Remember when that fella come here from Hollywood?"

"Dressed all fancy-like. Sure. I remember."

"Well, he never liked to come into town, don't you recall? An' whenever he did, he was always spouting off them ferrin' words and such." *Poor Tuminov. Him an' his wife weren't really so bad as everybody made out. They was just…different. That was all.* "Just too bad 'bout that fire that took 'em from us."

"Somebody ought to go tell, um, You-Know-Who. Don't you think?"

"Not me. Boy, howdy, not me." Heyes said with a low voice. "Besides, he probably knows already. You know how he is. He sees everything."

"Yeah," Chuck whispered, looking around. "I know how he is. For sure. I know. He sees everything."

*   *   *   *   *   *

As Lou approached the old Willow Switch rail station, she remarked to herself how clean the place was: no trash, lawns and shrubs trimmed, nothing overgrown or out of place to be found anywhere. *Not many people about either, but maybe that's normal. I'm used to crowds and finding people everywhere I go. It's different here. Slower? Maybe that's why there aren't very many people about?*

Smiling to herself, she ducked into a chicken restaurant down the street from the library, deciding to escape the heat, get some lunch, and try again to get some clues. *I feel like Vera from that Scoopy and Shabby cartoon! No. Scratch that. Vera was too smart. So, maybe I'm Delphina – a very clueless and clumsy Delphina. Too bad the Mystery Club isn't scheduled to show up to give me a hand,* she giggled to herself.

She wasn't very hungry, and "broasted chicken," whatever that was, didn't sound very appetizing. But a friendly older man, missing half his teeth was very convincing. "It's like yer deep-fried, but we got a pressure-cooker thang, like that Kentucky Colonel place does in Bixby. It's real good. Trus' me." His face twitched oddly as he spoke. Then, suddenly standing at attention, he recited, "Broasted chicken at Mom's Chicken Shack: Once you've had it, you won't go back." Lou glanced around, finding the quote to be the motto written on the sign, the door, the tables, and even the napkins.

She smiled politely and decided to meet him halfway with a fried chicken breast sandwich, extra lettuce, and tomato, and wasn't too disappointed. The sweet tea was the best, though. *Instead of advertising chicken with sweet tea on the side, they should be advertising their sweet tea with chicken on the side!* She thought, giggling to herself as she finished.

As she paid the bill, Luvenia decided to be bold, "Can I ask you something about Willow Switch, sir?" To his confused nod, she asked a variation of the same question she'd been asking everyone she met. She changed it up a bit each time, hoping to hit on the right formula that would give her the clue she needed.

And again, the only answer she could get was a reference to Reverend Bobby-Ray Beatty's yearly Gospel Revival, currently setting up down by the bus station. But this time, she sensed something in the reply, as if the proprietor was relieved to be able to mention the reverend's revival. Puzzled and disappointed again, Lou dismissed the feeling, gathered up her purse, and left the chicken place, steeling herself to keep up her investigation.

"I tell you, Ma," her son said reverently, to the picture hanging on one wall. "First that foreign fella comes to live here and his house burns down. Then most of the hobos what used to stop here, to help us out, tradin' odd jobs fer food, quit comin' by. Those bikers come roaring into town that one night, then disappear all sudden-like. Now we gots us a darned tourist? Somethin's changed," he said with a slight twitch. "I gots a funny feelin' now, ain't been there before."

*   *   *   *   *   *

"Ize jes goofin' 'round, Dougie! Re'lly! Ya don' gotta take it like dat, now!" Smitty pleaded as Dougie maneuvered to cut off an easy exit from the darkened alley behind the steakhouse. Normally Smitty found enough cans and bottles around town, to turn in for a bit of drinking money. But scrounging had been difficult lately, so he'd decided to save what little money he found and sneak around the back of the steakhouse. *They's always tossin' out bottles with a few drops in 'em.* Smitty hated to have to stoop so low, but needs must, as they say. *Yep. Things is changing in Willow Switch. Things are quieter. Fewer people are about lately, too. Something hapnin', I expect. But it ain't no business o' mine,* he thought bravely, remembering that several of his friends had gone missing in the last month.

Might Dougie be the one responsible? Couldn't be! I've known little Dougie since he was about knee-high to a... well, knee-high to an elephant, anyway. Sure, he liked to push his weight around a bit, but Dougie never seemed to be the type to do anything crazy. "Ize' jes comin' in fer a cold one, bein' so hot an' all today," Smitty tried to explain. Dougie's large size and menacing look was giving him chills, bringing desperation into his voice. "No need fer roughin' me up. I'll be on m' way real peaceable-like. Honest! Really! You don't-"

Smitty lunged away, now frantic, but Dougie was faster, and caught him easily, clouting him on the side of the head. Smitty's last thought, before unconsciousness overtook him, had to do with Dougie's breath. It reminded him of several other men in town with similar breath, and how they all had that same sinister way about them.

Throwing the limp body over his shoulder, Dougie smiled, knowing this one would be deemed as food for the thrall and his kind. He was tempted to go ahead and break the man's spine now but knew the Master wouldn't like that. He always wanted to meet everyone, before they were put into service. Dougie wiped the drool off his chin, as he walked to his truck. *This one might be a bit stringy. Probably taste like pickled jerky. But I like a bit o' chew to 'em.* The drive over to the lair wouldn't take long.

Entry 20:
My second day turned out much better. I woke up well rested, found a diner down the street that made excellent French Toast and spent most of the day wandering around town. I got a few odd stares, but nothing like the "Oh, another tourist" looks I expected.

Willow Switch is so tiny, I think saw most of it by mid-day. I talked to a few of the locals and visited the site of the new clinic. The people were friendly enough but seemed a bit tense. And I think the article I read about the research clinic might have been old news because the building looked almost finished. The hospital wing was already taking patients. It looked like they were holding a motorcycle convention on the construction side, but I couldn't see anyone except for the construction workers, going about their business. (This doesn't seem like the sort of place to have so many people interested in motorcycles. And I don't think I noticed any automotive stores around town. Just a single-bay gas station located near the Diner.)

I'm not sure what I was looking for. I'm no detective. I don't even know how to talk to people, to get them to open up like a reporter might do. I did see welcome mats at every doorstep, but otherwise, there was no sign of the monster or his minions.

I'm tired, my feet are sore, and I need a hot shower. I've never done so much walking in one day! Was basic training ever this hard?

Besides the new medical facility, I went by the library, the hardware store, and the courthouse. They all matched the places I'd seen in my dreams, but I didn't see any of the people. I even went out to the burned-out Tuminov place. Not that any of it mattered. Even a selfie with the monster himself wouldn't be any kind of proof for anyone but me.

This is so frustrating! I need some sort of evidence I can show Dr. Spacer, proving I'd experienced all of this in my dreams, that I wasn't just making it all up or suppressing some old memories. I need solid documentation or incriminating pictures. I need dead bodies!

(Ew! I hope I don't really need dead bodies. That would be gross!)

So, I've come back to my room with some soup and a cornbread muffin, ready to call it a day.

A relaxing, enjoyable, but very frustrating day. Tomorrow, I'll have to get back on that dreadful bus.

~~Good night.~~

Wait! What was I thinking all day? How could I have been so stupid? No wonder I couldn't find anything today. I was looking for vampire clues in the DAYTIME!!! Urgh!

CHAPTER 17

Juggling the books and lunch bag in his hands, trying to open the door with his elbow wasn't easy, but he was managing. Just then, Deputy Reed tried his best to step aside, as a petite, young woman rushed up to him, stopped, and huffed impatiently. "Oh! I beg yer pardon, Ma'am," Deputy Reed said, surprised, almost having been run over. Although surprised to encounter a visitor, he didn't use it as an excuse to be rude. "Here. Lemme get that door for you." Besides, she was cute!

"Name's Tom. Well, Deputy Reed actually," he stumbled out, as she passed him. Looking back, she realized her rudeness and paused.

"I'm sorry. I've just got a lot on my mind." She said pleasantly. "Thank you, officer." With that, she turned from him and made for the study desks.

"Deputy," he corrected in quiet disappointment as she walked away. He purposefully readjusted the stack he still held, groaning to himself. *How awkward was that, right? Why do I have to be such a dork all the time? Couldn't even tip my hat. I wonder what she's doing here, anyway.*

Approaching the main counter, he said, "Hey, Doreen. I got yer lunch here."

"Thanks, Tom. Just put those books down in that bin right over yonder. I'll get to 'em shortly." She sighed.

"Something wrong, Doreen?"

"Oh, nothin' much, Thomas. Just that odd girl Abigail, darn her. We haven't been able to find a replacement, since she just up and quit on us. It was her job to sort through and put away all the books folk turned back in and clean stuff up and all." She said, picking up the white paper sack, looking inside at what could only be foil-wrapped cornbread from the Chicken Shack, down the street. When the smell of fried chicken hit her, she raised an eyebrow and asked, "Did Clyde send this over himself, or did you?"

"Oh, yeah, well, sure. Yeah. Sheriff Lange said I should...." He trailed off. Doreen was one of those women that could pin a guy to the wall with a look, and she'd just made an insect display out of Deputy Reed – label and all.

"Thomas Reed, you are the absolute worst liar I have ever met. Your boss knows fried chicken and cornbread's my favorite. But not once in six years, has he ever thought to have 'em sent to me in the middle of the day." She said slowly, for emphasis.

"You know, I've known you since I was in High School when I used to come over to babysit yer little sister - God rest her soul. And I've never known you to be one to resort to fibbin'," Doreen narrowed her eyes and asked, "What is it you're coverin' up, Buckaroo? You tell me right now, do you hear?"

"I'm sorry, Doreen. Yeah, I was the one that bought it for you." Reed said bashfully. "I just felt bad for you, and I didn't know what else to do. What with the two of you breakin' up and all. And besides, I don't know what's gotten into the Sheriff lately. I've been coverin' for him all over the place -more than usual."

Deputy Reed leaned in as he said, "Up until a little while ago, I never could find him, on account of him always bein' off fishin' or some such. But now he's been in the office every day for the past few weeks. Not only that, he comes in early and leaves later'n me!" Doreen leaned closer. "I'd think he was sleepin' at the station, except his car's parked different every day. Funny thing is, he's still just as unavailable as ever, not doin' any more than when he was out fishin' all the time.

Once started, it all came out in a rush, "An' all them shady-lookin' guys he just hired, have you seen 'em? O'Dell tells me they was some of the bikers what came into town last week. Rode in real late. Started lookin' like they might make trouble out at Joe's.

"O'Dell gets there, sees how many of 'em there are, and calls the Sheriff for backup. Well, Clyde comes out there with Dougie and

Dwight, and a couple of other guys from town. But then he tells O'Dell to go back to his patrolin'. Like all them bikers are going to just quiet down and listen to him and a handful of guys - none of them deputies. I mean, O'Dell said there must have been at least twenty o' them bikers. But the next thing you know, the bikers are gone. Then a day or two later, this bunch of new fellas shows up at the station!"

"That is strange. I hadn't heard nothin' about any bikers," she said. "I did hear the new hospital got a new batch of workers over there, though."

"Well anyways, like I was tellin' you on the phone the other day, they all been deputized, same as me," he said, folding over the corner of his library card. "But you can't tell me they's real deputies! An' they're doin' all the patrollin' and such, me an' O'Dell used to do, too. In fact, he and I ain't got nothin' to do anymore, 'cept run all the Sheriff's errands. O'Dell don't mind much – he's always been a bit laid back. Bad enough I used to be the one the Sheriff would pick on to do all that stuff before. But now that we've got some new people on the force, it really chaps my hide!"

"Well, don't let that bother you none," Doreen said, placing her hand on his. Smiling at him, she fluttered her eyes as she said, "That just leaves you more time to check out...some books."

Every fiber in Deputy Reed's body jumped, except for his hand, which decided to freeze itself in place. He wasn't prepared for this! His mind went wild, trying to evaluate the situation, but failing to grasp a correct response. *Oh, Gees! What do I do? I've never thought of Doreen like that. Have I? Well, I guess, but... Now here she is getting all friendly! I mean, she's always been the Sheriff's girl! I just never considered..., at least not since high school. But....*

Deputy Reed, confused and stammering, realized the only thing he knew for certain, was that he needed to get out of there. He could think it over later. "Well, I got to go. I'll call you later, okay" He said, politely excusing himself. *I don't want to leave hurt feelings or nothin'.* "I got more things the Sheriff wants me to do." *Not exactly lying.* He left as fast as he could, trying not to show the weakness that had suddenly developed in his knees.

I'll call you later? Well, of course I will. Doreen and I talk all the time: on the phone, at the library, walkin' her home from church. Heck! We talk all the- I mean, it's just so corny, right? "I'll call you later." What a dork!

*   *   *   *   *   *

Entry 21:
Well, crud! Now I'm in trouble.

I stayed up and quietly slipped out of my room, in order to skulk around town after hours, keeping to the shadows as much as I could, searching for the evidence I need.

I'm not exactly a ninja or anything, and I was already tired by the time the sun went down. By the time the sun came up, I was dragging myself into my room absolutely dead, cussing myself out for being such an idiot as to think I could find anything substantial by myself.

I walked ALL night and only saw 2 people out late. They were sitting at the station, over by the library, making out. (This didn't strike me as very romantic, but what do I know about relationships, right?) Other than that, nothing.

I figured I could get in a couple of hours' sleep and catch the noon bus. Maybe make up a bit more sleep on the bus, too. But I slept through my alarm and didn't wake up until almost one o'clock!

So, I grabbed up all my stuff, as fast as I could, and rushed down to the bus station, hoping to catch something headed in the direction of the Little Rock Air Base. If I could just report in there by reveille, I'd be safe. Getting to the Air Base, I'd be able to give an account of myself and maybe spare an AWOL mark on my record. If I could, it would just be a slap on the wrist for being late to my final destination.

The station attendant was putting up the closing sign just as I got there. He told me all of the scheduled buses had come and gone already. Willow Switch didn't have a taxi service, either. The next bus leaving Willow Switch wasn't going out before 8 am. Nothing left to do but wait. Boy was my C. O. going to chew my ass!

I'M SO ANGRY WITH MYSELF! URGH!

So, too upset to think, I wandered over to the Library to pass the time and write this stuff down. (Well, maybe wandered isn't the right word. Actually, I was so self-absorbed in my self-abuse, I wasn't looking, and almost knocked over a police officer at the entrance.) I figure one more night in the hotel won't hurt anything, then I'll strike out for the early bus in the morning.

Entry 22:
Something about the silence of a Library, and all that frustration, but I fell asleep for a few hours (except for a slight kink in my neck, I'm feeling a lot better). It's almost closing time, but I've recalled some bits of stuff from my dreams I never wrote down. I'd like to get these things on paper before the Library closes. I'm hungry, but I'll go get dinner afterward.

There were times during these dreams, when I could see other things, things that flashed through my head, things from another era, similar to what the monster experienced when he first emerged. They had to be from the monster's memories. But they're disjointed and disconnected as if he'd lost them. And I think the monster has been spending time each day, meditating, forcing these memories to surface, trying to regain and piece them together.

Whenever he did this, these memories seemed to be all over the place. But each time, he would re-apply himself, trying to put them in order and make sense of them. Some were put together this way and now stand as events, rather than pictures and feelings. Others still seem lost to his reach, or out of sequence.

Ironically, his earliest memories were of waking without memory and being attended to by monks in an old monastery. They asked him many questions, but he could not tell them anything, as he did not remember. They, however, always withheld answering his question, "Where did I come from?"

Thinking him an innocent, they called him Adam and proceeded to treat him gently, teaching him about the world outside. When they shared their holy scriptures with him, he was not able to speak, which they took to be reverence. Although he kept it to himself, he was puzzled that he could clearly recall every word of the scriptures, but he could recall nothing else of his past. He also hid the pain that touching the Bible caused him.

Although the monastery could not boast the largest of libraries, its shelves held the widest variety of texts from all over the world. The new Adam read every manuscript the monks could bring him. Only one text, the word of God, had a power he could not understand. While touching it brought him pain, any attempt to read it felt like placing his face into a raging fire. His mouth bled if he attempted to quote the words. He could listen but was powerless to speak. And yet he knew every word.

That these men that cared for him, studied the word of God so incessantly, believed it so thoroughly, prayed to their God about it, and strove to live it so completely, both confused and amused him. They studied it as a historical text, as a vision and map for the future, and as a guide for living in the present. Their existence revolved around it as naturally as breathing. They experienced no frustration or doubt, but knew it to their marrow, to be the absolute truth. The new Adam understood, too. For even as their devotion amused him, he also knew the truth. Though written by a man's hand, the words in their scriptures were the actual, living words of the one and only deity ever to exist.

One day, finally responding to his frequent requests, the brothers invited him on a supervised visit to the upper levels, and a short journey outside. During the climb up the stairs, though excited by the prospect of seeing the outside world, he became frightened as he ascended to the ground levels. Then he began to feel sick and bled from his ears and eyes. The sunlight was only indirect and diffused, but its effect was powerful. The light of the sun took his strength, and he faltered. He alone understood the reason: to walk in the sun would be the end of him.

They continued to care for him and tried their best to keep him in good health. But he only grew weaker, until the day he caught a rat in his cell. There was something about it that drew him. He held it, studying it. Then it bit him. Experiencing anger for the first time, since he first became aware, he surprised himself as he bit it in return, sinking his teeth deeply into its flesh. The moment he had his first taste of blood, everything changed. He felt invigorated and energized, causing him to secretly catch rats throughout the monastery. He took them back to his cell, where he drained them of their blood and hid their bodies in a hole he dug out beneath his pallet of straw.

The day he overheard the rat-catcher, worriedly explaining to the Abbot, why his quota for rats had declined (he was paid per carcass), and how he had so many children to feed at home, thoughts of the future began to blossom. Here was a man quite unlike the monks, the only human representatives Adam had met. This catcher of rats did not follow the teachings of the sacred scriptures, as did the monks. Looking beyond the veil of the man's eyes, Adam saw self-preservation, self-doubt, and greed; all elements capable of corruption. Adam considered this. If the world were filled with creatures like this, rather than those immersed in the holy texts, dominance should be easy. And who more worthy of dominion than himself? So the monster bided his time, waiting for an opportunity to leave them, to strike out on his own, to begin building an empire worthy of his power and intellect.

His planning and speculation ended, however, when one of the brothers discovered the desiccated rat bodies hidden in his secret hiding place. The monks, those brothers that he only knew to be kind and gentle, became the cruelest of masters. Where they had once thought him to be an innocent, like a child in a man's body, they now knew him to be a heretic and a deceiver. They proceeded to interrogate him, putting him through tortuous trials, attempting to purify him through pain.

They stretched him on the rack. They tore and flayed his skin. They burned his flesh with brands of fire. They even pulled the nails from his fingers and the teeth from his head. They read to him from their holy scriptures day and night. Many times, he wanted to cry out or blaspheme against them, but he could not. "Where the Word of God is spoken, evil can make no sound," said the Abbot during one session. The torture went on for weeks. They gave him water to drink. But they had blessed it, so it only burned his throat and made him vomit blood. Starved, dehydrated, flayed, and burned, his body a wreck, he'd come to entertain that perhaps it might not be possible for him to die. After all, who could stand this level and length of torture and still have breath in his body?

After 40 days, his captors conceded this purification by torture, recommended by the churches in Spain, had not accomplished its objective. Shortly before the midnight hour, they brought him up the winding stairs for the second time. As he emerged from the building, he saw the platform of piled wood in the night's darkness, crouching like a mongrel dog in the center of the courtyard. And he knew their intentions. They staked his shredded body out over the neatly piled wood, as they prayed over him, pleading to God. Even as he faced the coming danger, confusion gnawed at him. They did not plead for his soul, as he expected. They plead for their own forgiveness. For some reason, they blamed themselves for his existence and his sins.

*Even as I finally get this stuff on paper, I'm faced with the same questions that the monster battles to answer: If the brothers and the monastery were his first memories, did they create him? Is that why they called him Adam? If so, how did they do it?

But this couldn't be. If his only memory was of the Bible, there had to be a time he existed before he came to the monastery. And, if he did, then where did he come from? Who was he before that time?

**Interesting. Now that it's gotten full-on dark outside, I'm noticing something lit up down the street, like a carnival or fair. But I don't see any colored lights or a Ferris wheel. I think I'll go check it out before I get something to eat.

CHAPTER 18

"Okay, Thomas. What's eatin' you?" Doreen said as she cut in front of him on the trail, stopping so abruptly that he almost ran her over.

Startled, he took a step back and looked down at his shoes, saying, "Oh, nothing. You know, work stuff."

"Work stuff, huh?" She stepped forward so that she could get her face up under his and catch his eye. "Bull-pucky! You've been as distracted as a dog with a bone, all afternoon. I know you got something on your mind and it ain't work stuff. Now, out with it, Buckaroo."

She was the only one that ever called him that, like it was her own special name for him. And Thomas Reed felt a tingling sensation as she said it. He paused a moment, recalling that he'd always felt that way when she called him Buckaroo. "I'm waiting, Deputy," she said, drawing out the word, to try to break his resolve.

Thomas Reed, dressed in one of his Sunday shirts and a clean pair of jeans, turned away from her, his boot kicking a rock that had made its way onto the well-beaten dirt path. "Well, gosh, Doreen. I don't know," he whined. Then she jumped in front of him again. He took a deep breath and said in a more controlled voice, "It's about the conversation we had earlier today at the library. It's kinda bothering me."

Feeling this was too important, she moved her head into line with his, so that he couldn't break eye contact. She thought she knew what it was and wasn't going to let the opportunity pass.

My goodness. She's so close. I could just lean down and... Suddenly, he took her by the shoulders. *I really could. I could do it. But what if she's not thinking the same thing? What if she doesn't think about me like that?* he thought. Then, desperately trying to push his feelings aside, he all but picked her up, moved her to the side, and resumed walking to their destination, Reverend Bobby-Ray Beatty's yearly revival meeting.

"Why, Deputy Thomas Nathaniel Hawthorne Reed! In all my years, not one person has ever manhandled me. Not my Pa, not Clyde, not anyone. But now you, of all people?" *Oh, crap! Now I've done it. She's getting riled and I've got to do something.*

He spun on his heel, almost knocking her down again. But his sudden movement stopped her in her tracks. "Look. I'm sorry I put hands on ya just then. It's just that I... Well, I just don't want to talk about it. Okay?"

If she'd stayed mad at him, he could have turned from her and stomped off towards the revival, as they'd planned. She might have followed, or she might have headed back home. But just as his harsh words came out, the look on her face changed to one of compassion. *She's not just pestering me out of curiosity. She really wants to know. It's just that she wants me to speak out the most embarrassing words a man can utter.*

I never should have told Sharon at the office. But I was mopin' and Sharon's such a busy-body. I couldn't help myself. I blame her for being in this situation. I never would have, if it weren't for Sharon's nosing in and making me do it. It was her idea I tell Doreen how I feel. It was all Sharon's idea!

Awe, heck. I can't back out now. "Yeah, I'm fibbin'," He said sheepishly. "You always know when I am, so I'll spill it." He took another moment to gather himself and said, "Doreen, you've always known me better than I've known myself. You knew it wasn't Sheriff Lange that bought you lunch today. It was you that knew I wanted to go into Law Enforcement and helped me apply for the job I got. Heck, remember when we were kids, sittin' there at our first revival? I really wanted to go forward with the others. I was ready to give my heart to Jesus. But I just couldn't move. I was so shy back then. I was petrified of anyone noticin' me and makin' fun. But you knew what was goin' on inside me. You took my hand and led me up to the front, so I could be Born Again. I'll never forget that.

"Well, it's just that I've known you since we were kids, and we've been like best friends ever since you started babysitting my little sister. And since high school, you've always been Clyde's girlfriend. So, I've never thought of you as anything other than a friend. And you're my best friend, what with the number of times a day we talk on the phone and such. But now you and Lange are broken up, and then you touched my hand earlier, and... well, now I can't stop thinking about, well... you know."

Doreen understood. She'd been attracted to Thomas Reed almost since they'd met. "Thomas," she said gently, taking his hands. "The only reason I started going out with Clyde was 'cause he was on the football team. With Clyde, I was popular and got to go to all the parties and such. After graduation, we kind of just fell into a routine, everyone just expectin' us to be together. Truth be told, we barely spent any time together. Until recently, I was just too stupid to realize what a waste of time Clyde was. Can you imagine if he'd ever asked me to marry him," she speculated, looking away. "I probably would have, and then where would I be? The only difference being I'd be calling him husband instead of a boyfriend!"

She looked up into Reed's eyes again and knew she'd said too much. *Should have just kept yer trap shut, Doreen!* Thomas Reed, senior Sheriff's Deputy for the town of Willow Switch, turned away in confused frustration and ran off in the direction of his house. "Don't go," she called after him, realizing she didn't feel like going to see Reverend Beatty's revival after all. *Maybe it's not too late to be the town cat-lady,* she thought miserably to herself as she walked back home by herself.

Entry 23:
Okay. I'm officially freaked out now. I've got to get this stuff written down and figure out what to do next.

The lights I thought were for a carnival, turned out to be Bobby-Ray Beatty's Traveling Gospel Revival, a tent as big a house, complete with a white-collared guy shouting out hell-fire and damnation. The same one that nice waitress – Libby – told me about.

The circus tent was filled with folding chairs, but a bit less than half-full of people. I thought the late hour in the middle of the week might explain the attendance, but from the preacher's reaction, he'd been this way before, and usually turned out a much larger crowd. He even made some scathing comments about low attendance during his sermon. He made the audience feel like it was their fault that more people didn't show up. A lower attendance meant fewer donations, which meant more difficulty doing God's work, which meant everyone in America was likely going to Hell. (What a jerk!)

He ranted like this as if he were the only evangelist that could save anyone. When he'd run out his anger, he took a breath, straightened his coat, and went on with his planned sermon, as if he'd not just spent the last 20 minutes berating them. (Like I said, what a jerk!)

"You have to have faith, my friends," the preacher said, starting slow and quiet. "Only faith can save you. Ephesians 2:8 states it clearly, 'For by grace you have been saved through faith.' Faith, friends. Faith!

"And only faith can save us!" he boomed. "Only faith can make us prosperous or fruitful. Remember what the gospel of Matthew says about faith: 'if you have faith as a mustard seed.' Faith, my friends. If you aren't prosperous and fruitful, it is only a sign that you don't have enough faith.

"If you don't have faith, you must scrutinize your own dedication. Without faith, how can you say you are truly dedicated to God? You, sir," he said, pointing to a random man in the front. "You, madam," this time pointing to a random woman towards the middle. With a wave of his hand, to take in the entire congregation, "Dear children, you are all back-sliders and in jeopardy of losing your salvation and being sent to Hell, come Judgment Day. Do you want to be thrown into the Lake of Fire? Because I tell you: that is exactly where the faithless are bound! Bound for the Lake of Fire!"

He turned away from them, pausing to wipe his brow and let his words sink in. He'd learned the technique in college, from one of the greatest orators of the 20th century: Adolf Hitler. The former leader of the Nazi party had a charisma that appealed to Robert, so he'd studied the old footage, over and over. The man's style and delivery captivated and amazed him. There was no need to understand German, to understand the obvious talent: bait-hook-net, bait-hook-net, bait-hook-net. "So, what are you going to do for God? How will you show your faith? Service? Do you feed the homeless, teach Sunday school, or usher in your local church? All these things are good. Certainly, your service will earn you treasures in heaven. But your service is not enough.

"God demands we sacrifice for Him, just as He sacrificed for us. He paid the ultimate price for us. Can I get an 'Amen?'" The congregation answered back, and he went on. "And God demands our obedience in all things, doesn't He? You know He does!" Bobby-Ray built the tension to a crescendo, before turning quiet and deeply serious.

Calling himself Father Bobby-Ray Beatty, Roberto Raymondo de Battallia Jr. loved using his talent, but he loved using others more. Little Robbie, as his mother called him, had come a long way. At a young age, he noticed that people tended to believe a lie if it seemed that you believed it, too.

But, after lying and cheating his way through school, regular jobs in the real world didn't appeal to him. So, beginning as a motivational speaker, he eventually hit on the religion angle, and Father Bobby-Ray Beatty was born, enjoying the freedom of the road and freedom from paying taxes!

"The Good Book tells us that our concern for worldly things, like money, is the root of all evil. The Good Book says that you must submit yourselves to God. He wants us to submit our time, my friends, our energy, and our thoughts to Him. But that's not all. In fact, the Good Book tells us to submit our finances to God, in support of His ministry and sharing of His word.

"My friends, let's be honest. You have responsibilities: homes, families, and children. You have stability and the assurance of safety in your lovely community. You have it good. Admit that you do. Sure, you desire the latest car, a bigger house, and nicer stuff. Everyone does. And we do what we can to remain humble in the eyes of God, don't we?

"But there are those, my friends, that have none of these things: no home of their own, no stability, no security. My ministry has been doing God's work for nearly 15 years. My ministry has spread the good news far and wide, across this fair land. But I have no home. I have no community to call my own. I have only God's work.

"So I ask you, dear friends, to sacrifice that which is dearest. Sacrifice for God's work. Dig deep. Just as Abraham was willing to sacrifice his only son. Give until it hurts, then give a bit more. If it doesn't hurt, it isn't a sacrifice, and that's what God wants of you. He wants your sacrifice, just as He sacrificed for you. Don't lose your salvation, dear brothers and sisters. Atone for your sins. Show God your dedication. Give all you can. Now. Tonight! I want to see checkbooks, my friends. Be bold, and not afraid, in support of God's work!"

Then, as the congregation bent over their wallets, he nodded to the men scattered around the room holding offering baskets, gave a signal to the choir ladies behind him, and began to sing out a chorus of "The Blood of Jesus. "

At this, two old ladies struck up the old hymn and several seedy-looking guys in suits began passing around offering plates. I watched them as they made sure to pause a bit more if anyone didn't put something into the plate. Some called aloud, shouting blessings for those they felt had given a large amount, shaming others into giving more.

Then a tall, well-dressed man, sitting somewhere in the middle, stood up and began to speak directly to the preacher, interrupting the music. His voice cut through all the other noise, as he asked why God needed money. The preacher looked up as the music stopped, but didn't miss a beat. He just smiled condescendingly, as if speaking to a slow child and began to recap his sermon. At that, the man interrupted him, louder and more forcefully this time. (Which was good, because then I really got to hear what he said.)

"You say that those who do not make sacrifices, that do not give to your cause, are doomed to the fires of Hell. Are not those who believe in Christ's sacrifice, as payment for their sins, saved from eternal judgment? Is that not what your scriptures say?"

Before Bobby-Ray could think of a proper reply, the man said, "Then how can a man who believes he is saved this way, lose his salvation? Would that not make God a liar?" Even from a distance, the vampyr glared intensely into Robert's eyes, seeing into his heart.

"The concept of money is a man-made invention. So, why give God money, of all things? How much must be given, in order to gain His blessing? Is there a minimum amount? Is there a percentage or calculation involved? Or should it simply be all that we have?

"And just what does 'until it hurts' mean? Are we to give away so much that we then endure hardship for not having enough to sustain ourselves? And you mention that money is evil. Yet you say that it is what God wants. Why would your God want something that is evil?" Father Beatty began to sweat, as he began to understand where this was going. His stomach dropped. Losing the crowd would lose him their donations, and force him to leave disgracefully and empty-handed.

"You use the book in your hand to shame these folk into giving you money. You even call it the 'good book.' Yet you threaten their salvation, and you threaten them with Hell. Do you even care to save anyone from Hell? Do you even believe Hell exists?" Now the hair on Bobby-Ray's neck began to stand up. This stranger wasn't just killing the mood and ruining the take. This was going much deeper. Roberto Raymondo de Battallia Jr. began to feel sick.

"This 'good book' you take such pride in waving about has those answers. If you would but read it, you would know that Hell is real. More than that, you would know that you truly could save hundreds like these, thousands like these, if only you shared its truth.

The preacher stood staring, with his eyes wide on this stranger. Apparently, he'd never imagined anyone would call him out so completely, in front of all these people. Many of them, like Libby from the diner, had attended his revival shows time and time again.

Even if he hadn't called attention to himself, speaking out against this preacher just now, the stranger would have stood out in any crowd. Tall and well-dressed, his voice was spiced with an odd European accent, unlike anything I'd heard before. His gestures and mannerisms seemed familiar, however. Then my heart threatened to stop, as the blood drained from my face and an icy hand clutched at my spine. This was the man whose eyes I'd been seeing through. This was the monster!

Outwardly, I kept my composure, but I wanted to scream! Now that I knew who he was, I was freaking out, and yet I had to see more. I backed out of the rear of the tent, where I'd been standing, and went around the side, moving quietly. There, I found a small slit worn into the fabric.

The man I saw exuded confidence, intelligence, and power. As he stood there, answering the preacher's feeble attempts to justify himself, I studied his face. Like something out of the desert, his face and body could only be described as chiseled and statuesque. He seemed to have a slightly olive-colored skin, but with a certain gray pallor, as if drained of blood. I couldn't help but feel attracted, even as I was repulsed.

Then the monster walked through those gathered there, toward the preacher standing on the stage. The preacher, stunned by his inability to fend off the monster's accusations, stood motionless, powerless to prevent this stranger from taking over his revival.

Gaining the stage, the vampyr turned to the rest of those gathered under the tent, "God created you to be with Him. But you sinned and cut yourselves off from Him. So, God reached out to you. And you turned away from Him. He even arranged for a piece of Himself, His Son to become man, so that the ultimate sacrifice could be made on your behalf. And still, you stumble, as if in darkness.

"He made it so simple. You don't even have to earn your way by deed or pay for it by death. All you have to do is believe that His Son's death paid the penalty for your sin. And His resurrection proved He is a conqueror over death. Accept this, and your judgment is passed over, and you'll be allowed to walk with Him. You will be forgiven all of your sins, no matter how many or how heinous, and allowed to enter into Heaven forever.

"I have studied your world. In your selfish ignorance, you pretend to follow your God but insist on disobedience instead. You spit in your God's face, and you actually choose to remain lost!"

The monster spoke to all those assembled. He mentioned what a shame it was, that so few understood the true power of the book they all claimed to believe and follow. They even called it "The Good Book." But their hypocritical lives proved otherwise. Didn't they realize they were holding the actual, living Word of God? They argued pointless details and tried to work their way into Heaven while missing its greatest message, that of salvation. The entire book, he said, described the relationship God wanted to have with them, even though they rejected Him over and over, insisting on doing things their own way.

This book was full of love, forgiveness, and sacrifice; God reaching out to faithless, disrespectful, self-centered, and disobedient, childish man. It was not about a disconnected "man upstairs," unconcerned about them. Rather, it was an attempt to redeem the fallen, to re-establish the relationship with Him, offering an eternal paradise He built just for them. Stupid, pitiful, ignorant man. How could He be so devoted to them?

From the podium, he asked if those present believed. Most nodded and shrugged – they thought they believed, didn't they? "No?" he said. "How could you be so unsure? It's all there, written in the Bibles you hold in such high esteem."

All this time and all these dreams, I'd only looked out from those piercing eyes, seeing the despicable, grotesque acts he committed without concern. Now, having heard his arguments, a shock ran through me. I knew he was evil, but he was also right!

I shouldn't have been so fixated, but as I stood there, dumbfounded by this now-confirmed reality, fascinated at how impressive he was, and shocked at a new realization, I failed to notice his minions and his thrall. They had taken advantage of their master's distraction, to position themselves around the tent.

The monster now looked at each of them, just as he'd done at the council meeting. I knew he was looking into their souls, looking for the corruptible, evaluating their usefulness. Through the small hole in the huge tent, I watched in fascinated horror. The monster's face changed in subtle ways, as he made his decision on each one of them.

I backed away slowly, never taking my eyes from the shrinking view through the slit in the tent. I backed away, for fear of being next, groping behind me, not wanting to trip over anything or make a noise that might give me away. I kept this up until the tent was very small in the distance. Then I turned and ran for the station, my only thought to leave at once. In my panic, I had forgotten the next bus wasn't leaving until morning. I'd have to spend one more night.

On the way back to the hotel, I tried to calm myself and walk normally, trying to plan my next move. On the bench, where I'd seen them the night before, again sat two people, wrapped up in each other, making out. But on a second look, I noted that one of the two was different from the night before. Why would a girl make out with two different guys on two different nights, on the same bench near the station?

As I locked the door to my room and reached for my journal, so that I could write this stuff down, I realized what was so familiar about the girl on the bench. When it came to me, I knew they weren't just making out. She'd lured someone out and was feeding on him. I know this to be true because I recognized the woman as the librarian from the second night of dreams – the monster's first thrall.

*Side note: I was surprised that the monster's explanation of salvation was so accurate, matching what Gregory was telling me: the heart of the Bible is the Gospel message. And, as much as I know the monster to be so very evil, just about everything he said was spot-on. If I didn't know how evil the monster was, I'd say he'd make a great preacher (Ugh. Maybe I shouldn't say that.)

And I have to admit that we ARE rebellious and petty, always resisting God's outstretched hand, insisting on keeping the Lord at a distance, rather than running into the safety of His arms.

Entry 24:
*This is more of a note to Dr. Spacer, than an actual entry in my journal.

The more I think about this, the more I'm sure I'm in danger here – or will be very soon. The town is real. The monster is real. And the danger is real, too.

If he's really a vampire (and I've no reason to doubt he is), he and his followers have just about taken over this town. In a matter of weeks, there probably won't be any living humans left here, that aren't under his control. If anyone here even thought I knew their secret, I'm sure I would be rounded up for food.

Even still, I need to know why he chose to build a medical facility here. Why not move to one of the larger cities? I have to know. But I also have to protect myself, or rather this journal. Because, what if something happens to me? Someone has to know this is real. Someone besides just me. Someone who will stop the monster from taking over...the world? (I can't stop him. But someone has to.)

So, I'm going to slip this into an envelope and send it to you, Dr. Spacer. I hope you will keep it safe until I return. (Or take it seriously if I don't return. In fact, if I fail to make it back, you'll need to give it to someone who can do something about this monster.)

I realize this journal isn't concrete proof, but maybe finding out what he's up to with the blood clinic will render enough motivation to get help.

By the time you get this, I will have been declared AWOL and MPs will have been dispatched to retrieve me. I just hope I can find some proof to my claims before then. (And hope they find me before the monster does.)

CHAPTER 19

Entry 25:
Things didn't exactly go as planned. (What an understatement!) Well, I knew I'd be arrested by the MPs for not reporting back on time. In fact, I was counting on it, once I realized I couldn't leave until I found out why the monster had gone to all the trouble to build a blood clinic in a small town. The MPs were a sort of safety net, in case I was discovered.

So, the good news: it worked. The good guys came to get me, just as I knew they would. And more good news: I found out a lot more about the clinic before I left. But that's where the good news ends, because I'm now locked up, awaiting review (luckily, this won't be a court-martial, but I could be facing some serious penalties, including demotion and being kicked off the project if my clearance is revoked), and what I found out about the new clinic only raises more questions.

From the outside, the main part of the facility looks functional. Not many people go in, but they seem to come out okay. So nothing suspicious there. One wing of the clinic is still under construction, though. The whole building is quite large for a place like Willow Switch, more suited for a large metropolitan city. But something about this place seems beyond the irony of a vampire building a blood clinic.

Crossing a newly repaved section of parking lot, where those motorcycles had been before, I snuck inside a temporary trailer marked "Office," and hit pay dirt. Hidden under a pile of blueprints, I found plans for a series of underground tunnels, a catacomb-like system reaching just short of the city limits, with access points all over town. Having access to such an extensive network, the monster would be very difficult to find, being able to easily elude capture if threatened. He could also use it to attack from just about anywhere, too. Most interesting, however, was the large room. According to the notes, it was set up for both water and electric and wasn't far from the clinic's entrance to the tunnels.

I'm no construction engineer, but I was impressed by the rate of progress. According to the attached notes, the majority had already been built, due to a crew that the foreman referred to with a strange comment. "As unskilled as these guys are, I have to give them some credit. They do exactly as they're told and handle all their own scheduling. If I didn't know better, I'd say these guys are all working 24-7, but their paperwork shows good rotation. Not bad for a bunch of bikers. Such terrible breath they all have, though."

Along with building and environmental permits, I also found memos regarding the clearance of state inspectors. Looks like someone's been greasing the wheels. I even found a copy of an application for tax-exempt status!

*I should mention that I've had to start a new journal, as the first is in Dr. Spacer's possession so that I can have something to keep things straight. I also think it prudent, to keep a record of what is really going on, in case something goes wrong. Moving forward, I'll have to be careful and hide this one, while I fabricate another for Dr. Spacer, filled with empty contemplation about how I'm finally coming to grips with my dreams and feeling more and more normal.

Every appointment is still going according to the same formula, by the way: "Let's talk about _____. How do you feel about that? And what about ____? How does that make you feel?" with the occasional, "Tell me more about ____. Could you elaborate?" What a waste of time! But I have to keep up appearances so that I can figure out a way to stop the monster.

Entry 26:
I've got too much time to think!

I'm worried about my job. (As lead programmer, I should be!) I'm one of only 3 people in the US, who can do what I do. My JAG is also working on smoothing things out for me. He says they might fine me for days missed and extend my probation, but he's pretty sure it won't go much further than that. The problem is the security review. If I lose my clearance, I can get shipped off to anywhere that needs a typing clerk.

Something else: My dreams have restarted. Things had returned to normal while I was away. But they began again, once I got back to my quarters.

The tunnels are nearly complete, and the clinic is scheduled to open in three weeks. Six weeks ahead of schedule, thanks to that group of motorcycle riders that chanced to ride into my little town. The monster smiled to himself. Knowing he had all the time in the world wasn't as satisfying as seeing plans come to fruition sooner than expected. *With the clinic running, I will be able to farm all of the blood I and my servants need, while allowing me the comfort of my own, secure realm, to be left alone to contemplate my future. Of course, there will come a time when I grow weary of the quiet life....*

Taking a deep, resigned breath, *But now I must attend to more important endeavors: I must rebuild my memories.*

"Remember," the Vampyr chanted to himself as he focussed, relaxing into his meditation. *"Cast back to the beginning. Focus on the darkness. Yes. I remember... I remember..."*

As the Vampyr's mind slipped into the past, the jumbled pictures and visions swirled: slippery, out of order, overlapping one another. He remained patient, however, having done this same exercise almost every night since his awakening. Sometimes, he saw faces that appeared out of the fog of his mind. Sometimes, long-lost voices or thoughts came to him, echoing out from memories that would not coalesce. They always seemed to be shrouded in fog, but the Vampyr was both patient and intelligent. Frustrated at first, the more he put together the clues of his past life, like pieces of a puzzle, the more skilled he became. He could, however, only go back as far as the monastery.

Memories from before he'd been named Adam simply did not exist. *Where ever I came from, whatever I had been or life I had led before I met the Abbott and his brother monks, was purposefully stripped away. And who else but they, would have done such a thing? But why would such pious men take an innocent man's memories from him?* He paused in thought, calculating and extrapolating the data. *Unless they were afraid. Perhaps those memories... Yes, of course. They feared the man he once was. Taking his past from him allowed them to start fresh, giving him back his innocence. This is why they called him Adam, the new man. This is why the earliest days were filled with learning.*

As he smiled inwardly at the thought, another random memory began to form. He quieted his mind and focused himself so that it would not fade.

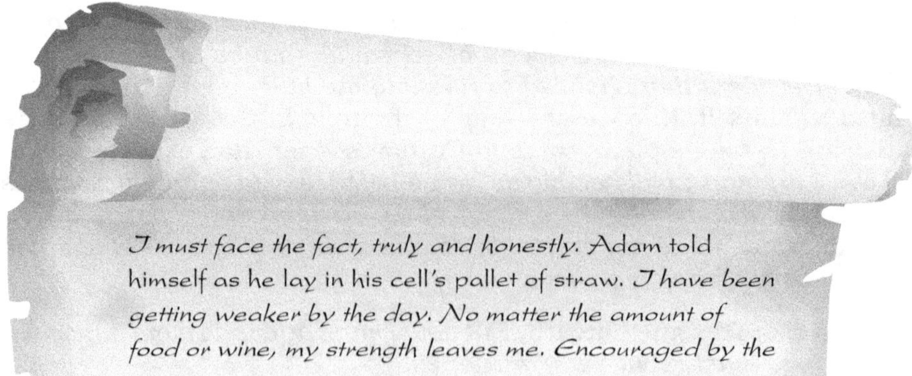

offer to finally see the outside world, I dared hope this sickness would leave me. But even God has forsaken me, as the barest of warmth and light that seeped through the passages above me sucked at my very essence. A few more steps and I know my life would have been forfeit. I cannot explain it.

Now, so weak I cannot rise, I must face my death. For reasons I cannot fathom, I have been brought to these men, to learn from them, only to die among them. Before today, Adam had not experienced sadness, but he experienced it now. Normally enjoying new learning, ideas, and emotions, he took no joy in this new emotion whatsoever.

Lost in his depression, Adam noticed a movement in the shadows of his cell. He had seen the rats before. They were usually stealing bits of straw for their nests, or crumbs of the food that served only to fill his belly, but not sustain him. This time they crept closer. *Perhaps they feel my emotion and seek to give me some sort of comfort in their presence,* he thought naïvely. *They are God's creatures. Perhaps He has sent them to me, to tell me He has not forsaken me after all.*

Recounting, Adam saw there was only one large and one small rat. The guttering tallow candle that lit his cell made it seem there were more. Smiling, he gently scooped up the larger of the two and held it close to him, petting its greasy fur. He was about to thank it for the caring gesture of coming to him in his lonely cell when it suddenly turned from him and bit deeply into his hand.

Pain shot through Adam's hand and up his arm. Surprise

traveled like an electric shock throughout his body. Enraged by the betrayal, he held on tightly, causing the rat to bite him again. Anyone else would have dropped the rat, ending the pain. But Adam was not any man. *Bite me, will you?* he raged. *Let's see how you like it!* As soon as Adam's elongated teeth sank into the creature's body, its blood gushed forth, filling his mouth. At first, Adam was surprised, but the oddly enlarged eye teeth that frightened some of the brothers were an efficient tool for blood-letting.

The coppery taste and smell overwhelmed Adam, and he drank greedily, sucking and savoring every bit that would come. Then he noticed his strength returning and it frightened him. He cast the desiccated body away from him. *What have I done? What foul thing has possessed me to kill so easily and to drink that which we are instructed not to consume?*

But even as he tried to come to terms with his actions, Adam knew the truth: the fresh blood had given him back his strength, as no other food or drink had done. Rising from his pallet, he considered his new situation as he hid his first victim under his pallet of straw: *According to the scriptures, the drinking of blood is an unnatural act. But it is the only thing I have found, capable of sustaining me. More rats will have to be found if I am to keep my strength. The brothers will not understand. I must keep this hidden from them. I fear what they will do, if they find out.*

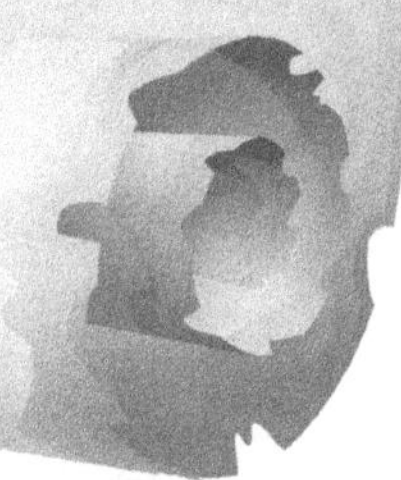

*   *   *   *   *   *

Interruptions, thought the Vampyr, *the bane of all leaders.* He opened his eyes. *So, I was once innocent of the taking of blood. But it coincides with memories of the brotherhood's comments about finding a dug-out cache of rat bodies as being the reason for naming Adam an abomination.* The Vampyr forced himself to push these thoughts aside, however, noticing the Thrall before him.

Rising from his chair, the monster placed a fatherly hand on her shoulder, "What is it, Abby? Why do you disturb my meditations, child?"

"I'm sorry for that, Master. It's just... Well, it's Dwight, Master. He's stopped talking and doesn't have the energy he once had. I... I think something might be wrong."

"Compassion? In a Thrall no less. Hmm...," The Vampyr said, speaking his thought aloud. Turning to his stack of periodicals and unread books, "This is not important. He is only as useful, as he is of use to me." Having selected the latest issue of *Business Now,* he turned to her, "Your friend Dwight is one of the more stupid of my Minions. He should have figured this out on his own. At first, any freshly killed corpse will do. But as they age, ghouls like him need older and older flesh, to survive." Staring into her eyes, he said, "Tell him to visit the local graveyard. He will find there, enough to sustain him for at least another few months."

As she turned to go, "Ah. And there it is. Compassion again, Abby?" She turned back to him and immediately seemed to choke as his mind slipped into hers, reading her thoughts, even as she thought them. She gasped at his power, having no defense, no way of slowing or diverting his invasion. "First that laughable novel you told me I should read. Now this. You really are my most tedious thrall," he hissed. "You have served me well, since that first night. But your tendency to compassion has always been your undoing."

Abigail Quinn fell to her knees, gasping as his mind continued to invade. "Remember the boy from your youth, the one that betrayed you into a life of loneliness? Remember how the adults treated you? Your parents and teachers, all wanting something from you? And you worried you couldn't give them what they constantly withheld. It was your compassion that betrayed you, Abby. And still, you hold to it?"

Tears filled her eyes, as she remembered. She could only acknowledge his words to be true. Why did she care about any of her Master's servants? Why did she care about anyone, let alone one of her life-long bullies? "I just thought...," she started, rising to her feet again, trying to explain away her concern, "the loss of one of us hurts your operation's resources."

"Abby, dear child," he said sweetly, moving to stroke her face with his fingertips. "It was weakness like this that made your life so miserable. It was weakness like this that allowed me to take you into my service." His eyes flashing and his voice turning harsh, he rasped, "And it is weakness like this that I cannot allow to continue!"

Abby screamed as her face began to melt. Clots of hair and flesh fell to the floor around her. She raised her hands to her face, to somehow stop the pain and push the bits back into place. But her hands and arms were melting too, her bones softening, the tissue becoming formless globs, barely resembling limbs. Abby's screams transformed into gurgling whimpers, as she collapsed, unable to stay on her feet.

She sensed the psychic call, as her Master summoned Dwight into the chamber. As he shambled in, dull of expression, void of intelligence, the Vampyr smiled, saying, "Sort out this stinking heap and chain it into one of the alcoves in the main passage. Make sure you display her artistically. I want all of my servants to see how she allowed her compassion for lowly creatures, such as yourself, to be her own undoing."

Dwight gathered up the crusted, now solidified remains of Abigail Quinn. In his arms, the pile of flesh resembled jellied dog food in loose, lumpy skin. But Dwight was beyond caring or emotion and did not notice that, except for the warped mouth and one wide eye at the top, she was barely recognizable as anything close to human. The Vampyr leaned close to what was left of her face, so that he could look into her one remaining eye and whispered, "I bound you to me because I needed your knowledge and access. You needed to serve me, to be whole. Did you think you could question me so boldly? You are MY servant. I am YOUR Master. I chose you to serve, and I choose how you will serve," he hissed as he straightened, his eyes turning cold. "And so, I now remove my blessing from you. From this moment and unto eternity, you will live as this formless mound of flesh. All of your senses intact, you will need neither food nor water, for I will sustain you myself. And you will rot there, unwanted and unneeded, alone in the darkness."

CHAPTER 20

Entry 27:
Lately, I've been thinking about the monster and his meditations. So far, he knows that he began life as "Adam" in that old monastery. He arrived there fully grown, so he must have had a life prior. But even in his time at the monastery, he had no recollection of anything before.

Most of his meditation sessions end with memories of his torture, his trials of purification. Although those experiences never fail to turn my stomach, I have to say I'm impressed, not only by the variety of methods but by the monster's ability to withstand so much for so long. It's no wonder he showed so little reaction when the Bible was practically burning his hand off!

Entry 28:
The monster's meditations have also concerned recalling the contents of the documents that were read back in the monastery. The name Moldavia came up, so I'll have to see if I can look that up. I suspect it might be the location of the monastery.

Yep. Moldavia is the mountainous region next to Transylvania, of all places! There are now a couple of apartment buildings, where a museum used to stand. That museum used to be a cathedral, which was the last remaining structure standing on the site of one of the oldest monasteries in the region, dating back to shortly before the fall of the Roman Empire. I even found a reference to this monastery as one of the major stops for Joseph of Arimathea – the guy that was said to have carried the Holy Grail to England.

In a related article, I found out that, once decommissioned and slated for demolition, all of the Orthodox church's old artifacts were purchased by the Smithson Museum, here in the US. Only one piece, a golden reliquary (an ornate chest with religious significance) was lost along the way. It had been fashioned after the Saint Niphon Cyprianos Chapel from the original monastery.

Authorities suspect it was stolen, as part of a smuggling operation active throughout Eastern Europe. The leader of which was recently sentenced to death, causing controversy over the enforcement of outdated laws, particularly in the country where he was arrested. I wonder if that might have something to do with the monster. But how could that relate to his appearance in Willow Switch?

While I was looking stuff up, I looked up the Saint Niphon Cyprianos Chapel. The website featured a picture of the saint in mosaic, from the vestibule of the church. Talk about déjà vu! I just about pulled all my hair out, trying to remember. I was sure I'd seen that image before. Then it hit me: it's the image on Grammy's pendant. (I can't wear it with my uniform, so I have it hanging on the wall over my bed.) It's a teardrop-shaped piece of ivory, wrapped in silver wire, with St. Ciprianos scrimshawed into it!

Entry 29:
So, I'm sitting here, thinking about my sister – probably because I started thinking about my Grammy's pendant, which has been in our family for generations. I'm the end of the Drukner line, so the family heirloom passed to me.

Most recently, my sister Emily had it. I don't think about Emily much these days, more out of self-preservation, I guess. Remembering is still kind of painful. But I don't have much else to do right now, and this journaling stuff is pretty therapeutic. So, I guess I'll take some time and try to explain. I'll copy it into the journal I'm keeping for Dr. Spacer. She'll like that I'm finally opening up about my sister. I did promise to tell Dr. Spacer more about her, so there's that, too.

Shortly after my 12th birthday, my parents died in an auto accident, and my older sister and I went to live with our Grammy. Over the next few years, due to the severe change in my situation and a growing feeling of disconnection, I found myself drawn to the Goth lifestyle, music, and everything. (NOT Emo, though! Please!)

At first, my sister helped out, as caring for two teenage girls was a bit much for a 70-year-old woman. But, as Grammy's health declined (emphysema, I think), Emily ended up caring for all three of us. She was so awesome, though. Taking care of us and working part-time, my sister still finished high school with a 3.5 GPA (fallen from a perfect 4.0). But it wore her out. I tried to help as much as I could, but I was too young to do much good. Besides, unlike Emily, and with the exception of computer class, school and I didn't seem to get along very well. I really had to work hard just to keep from failing. So, I just tried to keep to myself and not make the burden any greater, staying out of the way as much as possible. Maybe I should have asked my teachers for help or started sitting with the smart kids at lunch, but I've always been so uncomfortable around other people. I also have to admit I was really ashamed of my situation.

Just before graduation, Emily and I had an important conversation. I told her how I'd decided to study computer tech in the Air Force, but was torn because I didn't feel right leaving her all alone to take care of Grammy. I really wanted to help, and now that school was ending, I could get a job, to bring in more income. But I also wanted to get out of there and get away from the hopelessness I felt. I was torn because I didn't want to take over taking care of Grammy (although it really was my turn) so that Emily could go to college. Emily always wanted to study medicine and had been preparing as best she could to be ready for a pre-med course. But I just couldn't bring myself to step up.

In the end, Emily decided for me. After a long talk and a lot of tears, she looked me straight in the eye and told me to go. She explained that she had Grammy's care down to a steady routine, and if she didn't have to worry about me, it would all be that much easier. She told me that Grammy sometimes used me to guilt-trip her, as an excuse to get out of doing certain things. "Besides," she said. "Grammy won't be here forever. I'll see about going back to school later." Deep down, I knew that was all a lie. We both knew it was my turn and that I was fully capable. I don't know why she did it, but Emily lied so that I could get away. After all the years of sacrifice, in order to run the household, she'd sacrificed herself for me yet again.

A few years after I left, Grammy passed away, and the settlement of her estate revealed some old IBM stock that paid off every debt owed, including medical, and had enough left for that pre-med course. Emily also found the pendant that our mom had told us about since we were little. Grammy had hidden it away in the bottom of her sock drawer, along with old family pictures and her late husband's favorite western-style bolo tie, with an oval disk of blue turquoise – he'd worn it everywhere he went, but she didn't want him buried with it. My sister sent the pendant to me since she knew I still liked all that old Goth kind of stuff.

According to all the stories my mom used to tell us, the Drukner family can be traced back to somewhere in Germany. Printing was a big business there, due to the development of printing technologies. Before that, they were somewhere further into Eastern Europe, around Romania, where they were bookbinders. Shortly before WWI, we migrated to France, then America shortly before WWII. Every time we moved, we had to leave behind pieces of our heritage.

The pendant is the oldest and most dear to our family. It should have passed to Emily, but she wanted me to have it. I've never seen scrimshaw as delicately and beautifully carved as this. Only two inches long, and slender like your little finger, silver thread wraps around it, partially obscuring the decorative religious symbols bordering the central figure. Saint Niphon Cyprianos was a scriptorium priest and is the patron saint of scribes.

After Grammy died, Emily was finally able to pursue her life-long dream. Being a diligent, driven person, she threw herself into her studies with a relish seldom seen in many students. Emily's passion and focus took her to the top of her class, but the pace she'd set for herself took its toll.

She called me one day during finals week, getting ready for one of her big tests. Admitting she hadn't slept in more than 48 hours, she sounded exhausted but excited. After hanging up with me, she took a hot shower and collapsed in the bathroom with heart failure. Although her roommate found her and called the ambulance right away. Emily never woke up.

I shouldn't blame myself. There wasn't anything I could have done, even if I'd been there. And everything was done that could have been done to save her. But still.... I can't help but feel somehow responsible.

*　　*　　*　　*　　*　　*

Entry 30:
Just got word that I got my security clearance back.
They docked me 2 weeks' pay for being AWOL, but
I get to keep my rank and clearance, and I go back
to what I was doing before. Of course, since I'd sent
my journal to Dr. Spacer, she had to put in her two
cents. She's recommended mandatory visits until
she deems otherwise. So, I'll have to be careful.

She also recommended I get a hobby. I convinced
her that continuing my enrollment in shooting
classes, would be sufficient. (Maybe she wasn't
paying as much attention to our sessions as I
thought.) I have to admit, I've never liked guns and
have never been much good with them either. But
the instructor, Master Sergeant Gregory TwoDogs,
is an interesting guy – and talk about a history nerd!
He's WAY into everything to do with weapons, past
battles, and war strategies. And I have to admit
that, the better I get at shooting, using the range
relieves a lot of stress.

Entry 31:
As I've mentioned before, journaling is becoming
a bit more difficult. Since Dr. Spacer read the
first one (obviously she doesn't believe me), she
recommended our casually scheduled, optional
visits are now mandatory (three times a week!). So,
I have to keep two journals now. The one I turn

in to Dr. Spacer will be full of reports on how my dreams are going back to normal, while this one's going to be used to organize my thoughts and plan my next steps (if there are any).

But before I can start thinking about my options, I've got to put the clues together:

- The monster is definitely a vampire (vampyr, in the old language), who came from the same area as my family ancestors. This may or may not indicate one of them had met the monster before.
- The monster, as we know him today, originated from the monastery. But we don't know where he came from before that, or where he was between that time and this.
- He employs Thrall, that are closer to the cinematic versions of vampires, and Minions, that are like ghouls. He's also able to enslave willing converts without turning them into monsters, by getting them hooked on being bitten by the Thrall.
- The blood clinic is probably designed to cure his disease, rather than spread it. But since his vampire cult needs fresh blood (and dead bodies – yuck!), I'm betting the clinic is there to attract victims and, therefore, resources - maybe it will be setting up some kind of system to make the blood last longer? I read once, that the human body regenerates its blood supply, which is why

people can donate every so often. So, it follows that the monster could set up a system where those designated as food are not killed, but… milked. Disgusting! But it makes sense.

- It doesn't seem like the monster is bent on taking over the world, only securing his little corner of it. Although, given the speed and stealth he's used taking over Willow Switch, he could easily take any major city before anyone found out in time to stop him.
- Regardless of his plans for world domination or not, he's already turned or killed more than a hundred people, by my estimations. Even if he stays in Willow Switch, he'll keep on killing, too – he has to, even with the above-mentioned milking system, in order to feed himself and his followers.

So, good news: the monster will likely stay in Willow Switch. Bad news: even if he does, he'll keep on killing. Urgh! I just don't know. I'm stuck without a plan. All I know is there's no way I can stop him by myself. I need help, but there's no way anyone will believe me enough to help me!

The monster has probably already gotten to the local authorities, so they're out. There'd be too much explaining and re-explaining to involve the military, not to mention everyone's first thought would be that I'm crazy. Besides, I don't have any proof.

Pushing this responsibility off onto anyone else would be next to impossible, as well as unethical. But getting help from someone that would believe me, like Greg, wouldn't be any better. Even if I was okay putting him at risk, I couldn't forgive myself if he were hurt in any way. Anyone that goes up against the monster not only risks death, but even worse, they risk being turned into one of his servants.

Maybe more research and a good night's sleep will reveal something.

Entry 32:
I remembered something I'd read about all those kinds of monsters being immune to stuff like bullets and other normal weapons. And it crossed my mind, that all this shooting practice would be completely useless if I ever had to face one of the monster's followers. What good would bullets do to vampires and ghouls?

That's when my brain jumped in the opposite direction. Monsters like these always have a weakness to silver. Depending on the legend, they might only be allergic, or it might be lethal. I'm not sure what it could do to someone as powerful as the monster, but I'm willing to bet it would do something. Worth a shot? (*Funny pun!*) I'm sure a few into his head, would at least slow him down.

And, if I could slow him enough, I might be able to put a stake in his heart, and maybe cut off his head to be sure. (Not every legend mentioned the stake, but they all agreed that cutting the head off would work.) I might even burn his body, too, just to be sure that I'm sure.

CHAPTER 21

Entry 33:

My shooting practice is going well. Realizing I needed to do more than just to blow off steam now, I signed up for some more intense personal coaching. I also filled out the requisition forms for my own sidearm. I'll pick up my new standard issue Sig Sauer P226 in 9mm tomorrow. It only carries 10 rounds, so I'll have to add extra clips to my list of stuff I need to get. Maybe a tactical vest or something, too, to help carry everything. I'm just not sure how many of the monster's minions and thrall I'll have to deal with, and I don't know if silver bullets will kill them. Although 4 or 5 shots each should incapacitate them enough for me to get by.

Which brings me to the silver bullets I'll need. I wish I'd taken my mother's advice and invested in precious metals over the years. I would probably have all the silver I need if I had. As it stands, I've had to plan out some orders through some local dealers and pawn shops in Colorado Springs. I'm trying to calculate how much I need, but I keep coming back to, "That's not enough. I need more."

Lucky for me, Greg is a bit of a nut when it comes to weapons, especially historical stuff. I'm not sure there's anything I could think to ask him that he wouldn't know. So, I'm picking his brain to teach me all about making bullets – Sorry. "Reloading."

I've probably mentioned him before, but he's kind of a big part of my life right now, what with us spending so much off-time together. Master Sergeant Gregory TwoDogs, on loan from the Army, is built like a cinder block wall! I can tell he's self-conscious about the scar that takes up most of the real estate on the left side of his face and neck – almost a Harry Dent sort of thing. (I used to read my friend's BatGuy comics when I was in 3rd grade, okay? Give me a break.) He's really sweet, though a little different, and seems a bit detached most of the time, but he really comes alive when we're talking about either historical weapons and tactics or the Bible. Although I'm sure he's my age, he looks much older than me. Most of the time, like when I've hit one of Gregory's hot-button topics, and his eyes are all lit up and he's talking really fast, I look in his eyes and I can easily imagine the way his face looked before the accident.

Also, figuring I might need to take off someone's head (Gross! I really hope I don't have to do that!), I bought an old Army machete in one of the pawn shops I visited when I was looking to buy silver. (Did you know the Ontario Knife Company has been making machetes for the Army, since WW2? Go figure.) As an extra precaution, I sprayed the blade with an industrial adhesive and applied silver leaf. It doesn't look very good, but maybe it's enough to hurt the monster.

*   *   *   *   *   *

"It isn't very well written. But after trying 10 or so times, I'm just going to declare it finished and be done with it," Gregory said, as he handed it to her. "I don't need a proofreader or anything." Finally looking up from his hands, "I'd just like it if you'd..."

Equally embarrassed, Lou quickly looked down at the single page, shyly avoiding eye contact. "Of course, I'll give it a look," trying to sound more casual than she felt. *Why am I acting this way? I've never felt... I mean, He's not... Am I?*

She sipped her coffee and buried her eyes in the page, trying to stop the thoughts that invaded and began to read.

Dear Mom:
I'm writing you at the request of Captain Spacer.
Please don't worry about me. I wanted to write
you before, but I'm just not good at this kind of
thing. I'm a little embarrassed to tell you that
Captain Spacer is the base psychologist. She says
people don't go to therapy because they're insane.
They go because they want to stay sane. Not sure
I agree with that. But I guess it's her way of
telling me I'm not crazy, and that's nice.

So, I'm writing you as part of the therapy. The
doctor is a nice lady and all, but she's all about
writing down my feelings. You know me. I've never
been much good at that kind of thing. What she
really wanted me to do, was to keep a journal.
But who has time for such things?

This is probably my tenth attempt at writing
this. It's frustrating. But I promised Dr. Spacer
I would keep trying. I'm not sure how successful
I'll be. But, like you always told me: always keep
your promise, never quit if it's important, and
always give it your best. So, I keep trying.

I've been back from overseas for quite a while
now. I'm sorry I haven't contacted you and Dad
and little David, when first I got back. I was
pretty messed up and needed time to recover from
my injuries. (And, before you ask, no, I can't
tell you what happened.) I'm not trying to make
excuses. I'm just not ready yet. It's all I can do
to keep writing. But you deserve an explanation
for my silence. It will just have to wait.

Your son,
Gregory

"I had a whole second page written, explaining about the helicopter accident, the Army Rangers wanting to pink-slip me, and my C.O. getting me this gig here at the base since I was still fit for duty. But if I kept that in, I'd have to explain why I was stationed a stone's throw from the Reservation and haven't been home yet. So, I threw it out."

"It's nice. I think your letter stays focused on the most important thing: that you want to come home. And you will, right? That's what you're working towards, with Dr. Spacer. When you're ready, you'll go home and reconnect. I know you will." Lou found herself about to lay her hand on his arm. Just then, a buzzer went off, telling Sergeant TwoDogs that the latest cleaning cycle was finished.

As Gregory got up from the bench and walked over to the auto-cleaner, Lt. Drukner watched him for a moment, trying to get a grip on her feelings. Realizing she was failing and definitely in danger of getting emotional, she slipped out of the room, telling herself, *I can't let myself do this. I've got to stay focused.*

Over his shoulder, he said, "I heard there's good a bistro in town. I've been meaning to ask if you'd like to-" stopping as he realized he was speaking to an empty room.

Entry 34:
Greg and I have been spending a lot of time together this past week, practicing my shooting and reloading, and talking about tactics and war history. The other night, we decided to take our conversation to the on-base pub after our duties ended. (Not a date, or anything. Let's be clear. I mean, I do feel something for him. It's just that I can't let myself get distracted from dealing with the monster.)

He told me more about the helicopter accident, that they'd been flying pretty low, to avoid radar, but had been fired upon by insurgents on the ground. A lucky bullet had found just the right spot on the rear rotor, and they went down in a spin, thinking they were all going to die. After they'd hit, he woke to find a fire starting in the aircraft's electrical, and he worked quickly, to get everyone out that he could. It took four trips, but he got them all out and into a nearby building. The insurrectionists found them, just as TwoDogs went back for the radio pack. As he was leaving the aircraft, it exploded, spewing fuel and setting half of his body on fire. Still smoldering, Gregory managed to protect the radio and get back to his guys. As he collapsed, they laid down suppressive fire, radioed in their position, and called for evac.

After that story, we both needed a pint. And, for more than an hour, we sat there talking and laughing.

Later, I noticed the unscarred side of his face suddenly turn bright red, and he started stammering. I thought he might be having a stroke! But he was just trying to ask me out to dinner – like a date! (I haven't been on a date since…. Does Prom count?)

Of course, there are problems other than the fact that no one's ever asked me out before - like the fact that I'm an officer and he's an NCO – a non-commissioned officer. I mean, I could just go out with him, and who would care if it succeeded or not?

Besides, with all this vampire stuff happening, why should I worry about getting into trouble, right?

But then, what if we hit it off? What if I let slip about my dreams? He'd probably run away screaming. Or worse, he'd want to come with me! As nice as having an ally like him would be, I couldn't let him put himself at risk like that. And when we got back (if we got back), he'd share in any of the trouble I'd caused, too. Or what if I came back and he didn't? That would be even worse!

URGH!! I just don't know!

He really likes me. I can tell. And, given different circumstances, we probably would really hit it off. I mean…

(Oh, my! I think I like him, too!)

*   *   *   *   *   *

Entry 35:
URGH! The more I think about this, the more I believe this is going to be a one-way trip. I'd rather not go at all, of course, just shoot him from a distance or something, right? But I have to be sure the monster is dead. Even if I can get through all the bad guys, there's no guarantee I'll be able to defeat the big boss. I just don't see any way this plays out, where this isn't a suicide mission. I need a backup plan, some kind of guarantee the monster will end up dead.

I have no idea how to make one, but I think I need a bomb. I need to be sure he's sitting front and center for the big firework show - it'd be terrible if he's gone fishing or something when it goes boom. I have to be sure, and I think a bomb is the only way! (The Oklahoma City bomber used a truck packed with explosives, and it only took out half a building. How much explosive would I need, to be SURE I got him? With the tunnels he's had dug under the town, I might need something big enough to level the whole place, just to be sure.)

My biggest fear, though, is me. What if I fight my way through, only to be seduced into his power, and turn off the bomb I brought with me? There's no guarantee I can resist. I mean, I'd like to be able to say that I'm strong enough to resist, but who knows? The Librarian was a decent person. A nice girl that just wanted to be accepted and attract a nice guy she could call her own – same thing any girl wants, right? She'd shut herself away because the town rejected her. The monster took advantage of this and got to her, feeding on her desperation and fear.

What hidden part of myself would he use to take advantage? Gregory?

Emily. If I were him, I'd use Emily against me. No matter how much I've tried to deal with it, and whatever successes I've had, my biggest regret is my failure to take responsibility for Grammy. I didn't step up when I had the chance, and it will always haunt me.

So, I have to be sure. But how? If fire all but destroyed him when the monks burned him alive, what would be powerful enough to work? Sunlight hurts him. Maybe that would kill him. But how do I force him into the sun? Even if I was able to blow up his tunnels, that would only bury him, not force him into the light. But something like fire, something like the sun.... What about something nuclear? The power of the sun, but up close and personal.

Sure, I work at NORAD (secret command center for lots of nuclear weaponry), but the problem is, I'm a programmer, not a bomb-maker. I don't even know what I'd need, let alone how to put it together. And it isn't something I could ask anyone to help me with either. (Although Gregory would probably make one for me, just to show off how much he knows about warheads! – funny, but no!). The more I think about it, a nuclear solution would be the way to go. But HOW?

Again, through all this mess, I keep thinking about Greg. He's such a sweet guy, so worried about his family, and how he may have let them down. I really wish I could take him with me on this. He'd be a real force to be reckoned with! But I have to do this alone.

*   *   *   *   *   *

"I'm so sorry to be cryin' on your shoulder like this, Libby. I'm just so worried, you know?" Doreen said into the receiver.

"'Course I understand, Doreen. You and him been like a pig and mud since you both was young'uns. Why, you've been quite the subject among all those lip-waggin' gossipin' types for years. Not that I'm a gossip myself. But I do keep my ear to the ground."

"What do you mean? People been talkin' about me?"

"Well yes, dear. See, you've been going out with Sheriff Lange for so many years, but spendin' so much time with Deputy Reed. It's got 'em all riled up. They don't know which way to look. 'Course I know there aint' no hanky-panky goin' on tween y'all, or nothin'." Libby paused. "There ain't, is there?"

"Of course not! Clyde and me have been goin' out almost every Friday night, and we ain't done anything more than playin' kissy-face at the drive-in. I tell you, Libby. I'm a good Christian girl, and I been savin' myself for marriage like a good woman should. But I'll tell you somethin' about Clyde: he's never shown much interest, to be honest. At first, I thought he was just bein' polite and respectin' my faith. But now I'm not altogether sure.

"The fact is, he was the kind that liked havin' a girlfriend but not of getting' hitched. He was never going to marry me, Libby. As for Thomas, well I've always liked him. He was always just so shy back in school. I guess, when it came down to it, Clyde asked me and Thomas didn't."

"Isn't that precious? Well, I for one, am certainly glad you dumped that rotten old Clyde. So, tell me about Thomas, then. You and him's not working out now?"

Doreen clutched the phone with both hands, "I don't know, Libby. Ever since the other night, when he was walking me to the revival.... Well, we had a kind of argument. I just knew he was goin' to ask out me on a real date but was reluctant to say so. Maybe he thought it would spoil our friendship or somethin'. Then I pushed him a bit too hard to spit it out. And since then, he ain't called at all, nor come by the library neither. I tried callin' him at the station, but that old bat runnin' the switchboard keeps tellin' me he's busy."

"So yer worried he's changed his mind and you're gonna be out in the cold, is that it? Listen, Hunny. That boy's been carryin' a torch for you since you two were littler than bugs on a branch. He's just gotta have a bit of time to gather himself. He'll come around. Don't you worry."

"Libby, you're a dream. I don't know if you're right or not, but it sure makes me feel better hearing that. How's the diner, by the way? Is Dougie giving you any more problems?"

"Oh, I don't know. I guess I'm going to retire, what with my regulars not comin' in like they used to and Dougie not helpin' out in the kitchen anymore. I've had to close up, Doreen. Just until I can find help, mind you. In fact, he's the reason I missed the revival."

"Closed? But you've been runnin' that diner since I was little. You can't close. And what's this about Dougie? Did he quit on you or something?"

"Oh, Dougie's fine. He's just moved out is all. Said he's goin' to work at that new clinic that's opening soon. Silly boy hasn't called or come by in a while, but I'm glad he's finally gettin' on with his life. Of course, the house is a lot lonelier now. But I'm sure, once he gets settled, he'll come around to visit me. My Dougie's such a good boy, you know."

CHAPTER 22

"What the hell am I doing?" Thomas Reed said to himself, almost turning around for home. Stopped on the dirt and gravel driveway, he clenched his fists against his head, "Come on, Reed! You know how you feel. How long have you felt this way about her?" But the little voice inside his head, the one that kept him timid most of his life, continued to nag him with doubt. *What if she doesn't feel the same way? What if I'm pushing us too fast? I never thought this day would come, but how can I do this? It would change everything, especially if she turns me away!*

"No. I've got to do this. It's now or never. We're not getting any younger. A man's gotta do what a man's gotta do." He told himself. *Gads! Have I missed any clichés? I'm such a nerd!* But he squared himself up and fairly stomped the last dozen steps to Doreen's front door. *Sharon was right. I've got to be a man and do this!* He took a deep breath, ready to call her name, hand poised to knock, but Deputy Reed froze. He couldn't think, couldn't breathe, couldn't move his hand to knock. *What if I screw this up? I really like her, have since school. Would it be so bad if we just remained friends? Urgh!*

Thomas couldn't go through with it. But he wouldn't allow himself to abandon his mission either. And so, he stood there like a wooden Indian in a drugstore window, as the door in front of him opened, revealing Doreen's startled face in the porch light.

"Thomas! Why, I thought I heard somebody out front here, but," now noticing his arm, frozen in mid-knock. "What's goin' on? Is something wrong?"

Reed lowered his hand and closed his mouth. Then, after a glance at his shoes, he said, "Everything's fine, Doreen. I'm fine. It's fine. Everything's...."

"Fine?"

"Yes! Yes. Everything's fine. I just came by to, uh, to...." he stammered.

"Check on me?"

"To check on you. Yes," he said, relieved to have been handed a reasonable excuse. "I just came by to check on you and make sure everything was...." Thomas paused, took another deep breath, and started again, defeated by the truth. *She always knows when you're fibbin', Thomas.* "Actually, I came over to ask you something kinda important. But I'll understand if you don't wanna, on account of.... What I mean to say is, it's important enough, but I'm not all too sure I should ask you."

Doreen waited patiently, hoping she was right, hoping he was going to say something that had been on her mind all week. "Take yer time, Buckaroo."

Reed blushed, his breath catching in his throat. *Why'd she have to say that? Now those butterflies are at it again! But I've come this far, right? I've just got to push on.* With another deep breath, he closed his eyes and started in, briefly imagining he was back in front of his bedroom mirror, where he'd practiced this very speech the last two days.

"Doreen, you and I've been friends since we were little. We've grown up together and been like best friends all this time. We talk every day on the phone, sometimes three or four times. Saturdays, I'm usually comin' around to fix this or that and have lunch with ya. We walk to and from church every Sunday, as well as all the church functions. And I stop by yer house my way home most every night, just to check you're okay.

"Well, back when we was teenagers, when you started comin' over to babysit my little sister, I kinda started seein' you differently. But then you started goin' steady with Clyde, so I just put it all out of my mind, figurin' you and him was goin' to be together and eventually get hitched like most people do around here." He opened his eyes to find her staring up at him. *She don't look mad. I guess that's a good sign.* But the more he looked at her, the more his mind began to go off-topic.

Doreen smiled a little when he closed his eyes again so that he could continue. *Come on, dear. I don't care if you have to shut your eyes. Heck. You could write it in Hieroglyphics if you have to. Just tell me!*

Another calming breath later, he said, "Well, anyways. I'm not sure why you and Clyde were ever a thing, 'cause he never seemed to treat you very well, like you were an old jacket or something. Seemed like he only had you around when he needed you, but left you by yourself whenever he had other stuff to do. You know?

Doreen waited quietly, desperately wanting him to just get on with it and spit it out, but knowing that saying the wrong thing could break his resolve. "So, anyways. I didn't know what to think when the two of you broke up. I knew it was better for you, but I didn't want you to be sad. Which was why I brought you that fried chicken and lied to you about it bein' from the Sheriff and all.

"Well, ever since the other day at the library, when you touched my hand, I.... Well, it was like I'd had cold water splashed on me all of a sudden. I realized you weren't gonna hitch up with Clyde after all, and all these feelings I had back from when we was in school just came rushing back!"

He forced himself to open his eyes again. *I can't go through life with eyes closed.* "I'm sorry I ain't called you this past week. I've been tryin' to sort things out." He almost stopped. This time, when he looked, he found tears welling up in her eyes. But her face was smiling, encouraging him to continue.

"What I came here to say, what I wanted to say the other night when we was walkin' the footpath to town, was that I like you, Doreen. I don't want to push myself onto you or nothin'. And I'll understand if you're not over Clyde yet. But, gosh darn it. You're my best friend. It's just that I can't go on hidin' the fact that I want to be more than friends. I always have."

Thomas Reed startled himself, having realized that, as he was finally declaring himself to her, he'd taken her by the shoulders again. He froze as she stood there staring up at him. Her tears finally fell streaming down her cheeks, as her gentle smile broke into the biggest grin he ever remembered her giving him. "Me, too, Thomas. Let's just forget Clyde ever happened and start over. Just like we was kids again."

"I'd sure like that," he said, smiling back at her. Then, putting on a serious face, "Who's this Clyde fella, anyway?"

Doreen laughed like she hadn't laughed in a long time. *He's still holding me. Is he going to kiss me? I hope does.* She thought, placing her arms around him as he took her face in his hands. "Doreen Switchelberry, I don't want to be your friend no more," he said, as he bent down and kissed her gently on the lips.

For a guy that hasn't gotten around much, boy can he kiss! Doreen thought, before asking him to come in out of the cold night air.

*   *   *   *   *   *

Frowning to himself, TwoDogs turned the page. *What the hell is she talking about? Even if all this stuff is true, why would she be thinking about making a bomb?* Tempted to throw the journal away, instead, he shoved it back into the locker. This was just too strange.

Turning away, he determined to think of other things and come back to this task after mid-day chow. He had other things he could be doing, and this could wait. *Why me, Lord? I find a really great girl, but she's an officer. We hit it off like we've known each other all our lives, and I think she might like me enough to break protocol and go out with me. Then she turns out to be a secret nut case?! This just doesn't make sense.*

Master Sergeant Gregory TwoDogs paused, gun parts spread before him, his gloved hands covered in solvent. He blinked a few times and reapplied himself to scrubbing the buildup from the trigger assembly in his hand. Normally, the significance of restoring General Rankin's newly acquired Civil War Army Colt would have taken all of Gregory's attention. Few things he loved more than handling an actual piece of ancient history. But he couldn't stop thinking about what the Lt. had written. *What if it's true? Could a monster, like what she described, actually exist?*

Twodogs got up from his bench and began pacing. *If it were true. If it were true. Think, man!* He forced himself to focus, switching gears in his head to think strategically, temporarily removing all doubt. *Think about it. If a monster like what she describes exists, she had it right. She wouldn't be able to get help - no one would believe her. She had to act or this evil would spread.* His mind went through the possibilities. *She'd need a way to get through the gauntlet, to the monster, as well as a way to kill this thing.* Thinking strategically, he succeeded in arriving at the same conclusions Lt. Drukner made. She would only have one chance, and she had to be sure.

And now the interest in reloading makes sense, too. He removed his gloves again and returned to the journal.

Entry 36:

I'm almost finished with these lines of code. They should provide a back door that I can access and activate via phone line, to initiate a "test fire" on a designated location. The system will replace the dummy warhead with a live Dandelion warhead. (The Dandelion is designed to fall from orbit, rather than fly by its own power. Being about the size of a bowling ball, it's practically undetectable by ground radar, and the payload is equivalent to between one and two megatons, able to destroy an 8-10 mile radius of impact - just about the size of a small town.) Activating it by phone is important, as I may run into trouble getting there.

As they are classified, not too many people would know that Dandelion warheads are part of a super-secret orbital satellite program, designed as a fail-safe against countries dabbling in nuclear weapons, countries that have no business playing with that sort of technology. If a government like this starts getting a bit too full of themselves, threatening their neighbors, just because they have newly acquired nuclear capability, the President can authorize a Dandelion drop and take them out.

For a nuclear device, Dandelions are almost laughingly underpowered. But they were designed so that the blast would look like someone mishandled their own device, and accidentally blew up their own facility. The warhead is fairly small, just big enough to take out a military facility (or a small town), but not big enough to cause very much collateral damage, such as fallout. The impact crater of the warhead alone is enough to wipe out most small facilities, so it could conceivably be dropped sans payload and still do the job. The bomb itself uses no propulsion or onboard computer guidance, to locate its target. Instead, it falls from orbit, like a piece of space junk. What really sets it apart, is the Pinpoint-V satellite's surgical calculation of the warhead's release – something we weren't able to do until recently, as the technology had to catch up to the idea.

With my clearance and know-how, hacking into NORAD's system was easy. Nodes that I don't have direct access to, aren't as protected as the brass imagines. The code, however, is a bit tougher. Also, I have to write it from my personal computer, without proper testing against the program. Stored onto a thumb drive, the first time my code will see the program it is infiltrating, will be when I download it. It has to be right the first time, as there will be no second chance. I'm also trying to work in a line of code that will act as a cover-up, so that investigators after the fact, will see the launch as a glitch in the system, rather than a hack. According to system records, a line of old test code scheduled a drop that was never canceled. And a second system glitch accidentally loaded a live warhead, rather than a dummy. It's a stretch, but it should protect everyone involved, including the Pinpoint program itself, as I think Pinpoint is a really good idea.

He stared into space for a few minutes, making connections and pulling out old memories. It seemed like Operation Pinpoint was something he should know about, but he couldn't quite put his finger on it. *Is that the project she'd been working on? Doesn't matter. I understand what she's done. Logical, strategic, perfect. Damn!* He thought with a wry smile.

Noticing there was more, he read on. Afterward, he asked himself several times, if he had it all to do again, would he have kept himself from reading the rest?

FINAL NOTES:
I'm almost ready. Once I am, I won't have time for any more notes. So, this will have to be the last one.

I do this for the greater good, naturally, but more so for my sister, who gave up so much for me. This may not make us even, but it's all I can do.

I think I'm going to put this in the locker I was assigned, down in the armory. Once I'm declared AWOL, and someone realizes that I was headed to the town that became a crater, the locker will get cleaned out. I'm hoping it will be Greg, but either way, the mystery will be solved.

So, if this is ever found by anyone other than Greg, please pass the following message to Master Sergeant Gregory TwoDogs.

Greg:
I know you like me, and I hope you understand how much I like you, too. I deeply cherished the long talks - even if they were mostly about battle tactics, muzzle velocity, and historical figures. Spending time with you made me realize how short life can be. We never know how much time we have here, to spend with other people.

If it weren't for the urgency of this personal mission, I'd have gladly broken protocol to be with you. Most importantly, I need you to know this: I never saw the scars, only the tenderness of your heart.

Louvenia Drukner, Lieutenant,
US Air Force, NORAD

*   *   *   *   *   *

"Oh, no. It wasn't anything like that, Libby. Thomas is a good Christian man. After I invited him in, we just stayed up late and talked. Well, in between kissing sessions," she giggled over the phone. "But we mainly just talked. I will have you know that Sheriff's Deputy Thomas Reed is a true gentleman."

"Well, that's good to hear, dearie. Lord knows you deserve better than that selfish old Clyde."

"You've got that right, Libby! You know it's amazing. Over the years, Thomas and I have talked about nearly every subject under the stars. But last night, I think I've gotten to know more about him than I have since we were kids."

"That makes me so happy to hear. Your poor mother, God rest her sweet soul, would have been so proud of you, you know that? Thomas is such a lucky fella. I'm still hopeful my little Dougie can find an upstanding Christian girl, too.

"Oh, my! Speaking of Dougie, I'm going to have to hang up with you, Doreen. Dougie's comin' by to pick me up. Said he was goin' to introduce me to his new boss tonight. I'm so proud of him, makin' new friends and all. My little Dougie's such a good boy."

* * * * * *

The Willis boys didn't mind hard work, but they lived to party. A typical week of odd jobs ended with beers at Little Joe's. But bigger scores would mean a trip to the truck stop in Bixby. These big scores never were very big, but the Willis boys knew how to be frugal. Bixby had what little Bible-thumping towns, like Willow Switch didn't, namely what truck drivers called "lot lizards." But the hookers that hung out at truck stops were avoided by most truck drivers, as their low cost and eagerness didn't make up for the fact that they were usually supporting drug habits and carrying diseases. The Willis boys, however, didn't mind the occasional trip to the free clinic, because these hookers were just what Austin, Beau, and Cody were looking for. And lot lizards were nothing if not cheap.

They also saved money on hotel rooms by parking their old, camper-laden truck on the outskirts of the lot near the truck stop. They took turns in the back of it with the local prostitutes, ate jerky and microwave burritos, and drank the cheapest beer they could find. When the money ran out, they'd have to head back home, and start up all over again.

Items stolen from the Tuminov place, coupled with a term in the county jail, had provided them with the longest vacation ever. Finally out of jail, they decided to spend the last of their money on a hotel room with two beds. (Of course, no matter what game they played, to see who had to sleep out in the truck, Cody lost every time.) So, broke again, they readied the truck for the trip back.

"You guys done packin' our stuff inta the truck yet? Couple o' lazy asses, ya ask me," Austin said around his beer, stretched out on one of the beds in front of the room's little television. After spending the last couple of months in jail, Austin felt he deserved to relax, while his brothers did the heavy lifting. "Don' ferget ta take the shower curtain, too. We can always use it like a tarp, fer when we're haulin' manure."

"What about the TV? Shouldn't we ought ta put that in the truck, too?" Beau asked, pointing his large finger at the tiny set.

"Yeah, yeah. What about the TV? We could put it in the bathroom at home. Like them rich folks do on that show! We ought ta put that in the truck, too," added Cody on his way out with the shower curtain.

"Not yet, boys. I'm still watchin' it. B'sides, yall ain't done packin' ever'thing yet. We's takin' the TV last. Got it?" he barked, showing his anger. *Not forgettin' 'bout all the trouble you got us into, Cody. Darn fool's always shootin' his mouth off, 'cause he knows Beau will pound anyone dumb enough to try an' shut him up. An' I tol'd 'im to settle down, didn't I? Darn fool. Got all three of us tossed into the clink!*

"Zat the last o' the beer?" Beau asked, looking at the empty cooler. "Gosh, Austin. Why'd ya drink up the last o' the beer?"

"Beau," Austin said slowly, trying to warn the slow man. "Yer jus' gonna get Cody all riled up again," he whispered menacingly.

Just then Cody poked his head back into the room. "Last beer? Was that the last beer? Yeah, Austin. Why'd ya drink up the last beer? Beau and me's thirsty, too, you know. Why'd ya drink up the last beer, huh?"

CHAPTER 23

Placing the phone back into the cradle, Louvenia took a deep breath. No turning back now. The trip back to Willow Switch, Arkansas was almost like a dream. Resolved to her mission, she'd tried to just keep focused on the trip, first packing the necessary items, then the trip to the airport for a civilian flight to Little Rock, and a car rental at the airport. From there, she'd driven straight to the Willow Switch Inn. Lou had decided to take her time, making sure everything was prepped and ready, before making the phone call that would start the timer.

She'd planned on checking in, grabbing some food, and taking a nap until dark. But she didn't feel hungry. She didn't feel tired. All she felt was queasy.

How can I do this? I'm no special forces operative, like Gregory. I wish I was, though. Urgh! The closer I get, the more nauseous I feel. I'm going to end up face to face with the monster, only to throw up all over the place! Yeah. That'll solve everything. I won't need to drive a stake through his heart or cut off his head. I'll just vomit all over him!

Difficult as it was, though, she decided to force herself to stick to her plan. Besides, sitting in her room feeling sick didn't appeal to her as much as trying to get her mind off of the task. She couldn't move forward with her plan for several hours anyway. As it turned out, she was much hungrier than she realized. Lou worried she wouldn't be able to sleep at all, too. But stress and a full belly made the difference. At her alarm, she woke rested, resolved, and ready.

Checking her weapon and securing the extra clips of ammunition, she panicked again. *Well. Why couldn't I just take off? I could run for the hills, and let Pinpoint do the work!* With a maturity she didn't realize she had, she shook off the sudden feeling, clinging fiercely to her more pragmatic self, and moved towards the door. She put her hand into her pocket, remembering the necklace. *Just you and me now, Saint Cyprianos,* she placed it around her neck and situated it inside her t-shirt. A check of her watch let her know there was no turning back now. The program she'd started with her phone call had already initiated its task, beginning an unstoppable countdown.

* * * * * *

Even with earplugs, her ears rang. Shots fired in enclosed spaces of the tunnels beneath the clinic were deafening, especially without the sound baffling treatments lining the shooting range. Lou thought she'd prepared herself to shoot the monster's minions. But this wasn't like any video game or firing range scenario. This was an actual person. So, when she faced the one she recognized as Dwight, she tried to warn him off, even as she pointed the gun at him. She almost didn't recognize him, with his sunken cheeks and leathery skin that pulled his lips back from his teeth. *What happened to him?* she wondered to herself, noting his reddened eyes. But he kept moving towards her, not heeding her warnings for him to just leave. In the back of her mind, she remembered the speed minions like him were capable of, so she panic-fired at his first flinch, emptying the clip of silver slugs into him.

He jerked backward with each hit, just like in the movies, and didn't fall until his back bounced off the wall behind him. Afterward, Louvenia felt sick. She felt the bile rising in her throat, fighting hard not to throw up. This was her first kill of a real human being. *I tried to reason with him. I really didn't want to. And, geez! It took so many bullets! I hope I don't have to go through an entire clip for every one of these guys.*

"Just stay down, okay?" she said, as she glanced down at the ejected clip, she noticed the pistol hadn't locked back, so she still had one left in the chamber. *I guess I should go ahead and change clips. Greg had called it a "tactical reload," right?* In the second that took, Dwight rose from the floor and again started moving toward her, his shirt oozing a dark, viscous substance. As he did, he checked himself, realizing he was actually feeling pain and moving much slower. The wounds hurt, his joints hurt, and his thoughts came slower, though still focused on capturing this idiot girl. The master would see him fed to the others if he failed.

Louvenia almost screamed as she slammed the half-ejected clip back into the pistol and fired. Staring at him, practically face-to-face, she'd just pointed at what she was looking at. She never intended to shoot him in the face, but it worked. Most of the back of Dwight's head found itself all over the wall behind him. The rest of him stood there for a long second before falling sideways, like a sack of potatoes.

Pausing a whole minute, before nudging him with her foot, she decided he was finally dead for good. *Headshots work. Well, that's good to know. So, I guess NOW I can put in that other clip,* she sighed. Checking her watch, she steeled herself. "Back to the mission."

*   *   *   *   *   *

The top-secret orbital weapons platform labeled NASA Orbital Research V, in order to disguise its actual function, sent an alert back home to NORAD base, confirming the commencement of test A-21-B. It then altered course and commenced dropping to MEO (minimum earth orbit), to test-drop a single, Dandelion warhead, per its program.

Back at NORAD, Corporal Danforth, more puzzled than panicked, followed procedure, hit the big red "feces targeting ventilator" button, and pulled his board, checking it for immediately detectable anomalies.

While the platform executed its maneuvers, internal calculations were made to target the impact sight, near a new blood clinic in Willow Switch, Arkansas, with pinpoint accuracy. By the time the satellite completed its course change, Danforth had concluded the problem wasn't with his board. At the same time that he reached to answer his phone, the calculation on board the platform had been completed. Long before Corporal Danforth could confirm the alert to Command, however, the live warhead dropped from orbit.

*   *   *   *   *   *

According to the maps she'd found, the tunnels ran under most of the town. The entrance she'd found behind the new clinic, however, wasn't far from a large room situated near the library, with a hookup for both water and power. Reasoning this must be the monster's residence, she made her way according to the schematics. *Did I just get lost? How could I get lost? I have a map, for goodness sake! So, there should be a turn or opening here, that takes me to the main chamber. Where the heck is it?* Just then, her flashlight came across a curtain of some kind, hung across an obvious intersection in the corridor. *Oh. Maybe this is it.*

Drawing back the fabric and stepping through, Lou almost tripped over a pile of junk on the floor, blocking the way. Nope. This isn't it either. This is only an alcove. Turning to continue down the corridor, Lou noticed movement from the pile, and almost jumped out of her skin when it made a high whimpering noise. Lou flashed her light on the pile, finding it to have a vague face-like shape on the top, with one eye staring out at her. Lou stepped back in disgust, as she made out the lines of what could only be described as a blob of flesh, formless yet understandably somehow human.

"That's just Abby," Penelope said from behind. For the second time in as many minutes, Lou just about jumped out of her skin, as she whirled around, ready to shoot, the voice coming from back the way she'd come. "She's probably trying to ask you to kill her, put her out of her misery or some such." Leaning to the side, in order to look past Lou, "Aren't you, you pathetic thing?" Then to Louvenia, "So disgusting! See," she continued as she boldly circled Lou, seemingly oblivious to the gun that was trained on her. "Our sweet little Abby got a bit too smart for her own good. BIG mistake! Not only did she show compassion for the guy you killed back there," she said, pointing over Lou's shoulder, "a guy that actually made her life a living hell back in the day, of all people. But she ALSO had the big brass balls to interrupt the Master's meditations to do so." Penelope Bishop, former mayoral assistant and now senior thrall to her Vampyr Master, sighed dramatically. "Once a smart-ass know-it-all, always a smart-ass know-it-all, I guess." She said, gesturing towards the misshapen thing in the alcove. "So, he did this."

An Army Lieutenant should have known better. But she was distracted by this woman's sudden presence and casual attitude. *Where have I seen this woman before? Oh, yes. She's the Mayor's assistant. I recognize her now.* Just when Lou dropped her guard and glanced at the thing called Abby, Penelope's hand shot out, striking the pistol, causing it to skitter across the floor. Lt. Drukner's defense training, brief as it was, saved her as she threw her arms up to protect her head and crouched. Then, as Penelope charged, Lou grabbed, pivoted, and threw the thrall over her hip. Recovering, she drew the silver-coated machete she'd prepared, in case she had to behead the monster. *Well, I guess a thrall is a monster, too, right?*

Penelope, assuming her advantage, slowly rose to her feet, brushing herself off. Chuckling to herself, she said, "Well, we've got us a fighter here, eh, Abby?" Just then, Lou struck her own blow. Not exactly accurate, her weapon chopped down on Penelope's shoulder, rather than into her neck. Thick, black blood poured out of the wound, soaking Penelope's clothing and dripping onto the floor, like old motor oil. Lou had prepared herself as best she could, for the fountain of blood that would spurt from a wound like this, possibly spraying all over everything. But this was different. This was a different kind of gross.

Penelope Bishop stared at her ruined arm, saying to herself in disbelief, "But the Master said nothing could hurt us."

Lou quickly chopped again, this time hitting the neck, but at a bad angle. *Crap! I really suck at this.* Penelope staggered, holding her head in place with one hand while reaching out for balance with the other. "Don't forget, I killed Dwight. Your Master is a liar."

Penelope let out a scream of frustration and gathered herself for another lunge at Lou. "No. This can't be--." This time, the machete cut the rest of the way through, toppling the thrall to the ground, her head rolling a few feet away. *I guess cutting off the head works, too. Ick!*

Picking up the fallen pistol, Lou followed her trained protocol and checked the weapon. Her watch told her she was quickly running out of time, before impact. *I have to make sure he's here!* She was about to resume her search for the inner chamber when she heard a soft voice from the alcove. Lou almost cried as she made out, "Kill me."

As disgusting to look at, as the monster had made Abby, Louvenia still felt compassion for her. Kneeling close, she asked, "I'm sorry. I know I just killed two people, but I just don't think I can. I mean-"

Abby closed her eye meaningfully, trying to move her face side-to-side, in order to communicate the negative, and repeated herself.

"Wait. 'Pray for me?' Is that it? You want me to pray for you?" The mass of flesh wobbled as if to agree, as the single eye on the top closed and opened. The misshapen mouth turned up, as if in a grin. "I'm not sure praying for you would do much good, if you're not saved. You aren't, are you?" The creature that was Abby shook a bit, side to side.

Knowing Willow Switch to be a very church-oriented town, Lou took a chance. "Do you know about Jesus, that He came to die for you, and that by accepting Him as your Savior, you can be saved too?" The eye seemed to tear up, as Abby wobbled in assent. "Well, why don't I pray WITH you, instead? I know you probably think you're beyond saving, but there's no sin Christ can't forgive. Would you like to accept Him into your heart and be saved from your sin?"

The lump of flesh closed its eye, as tears streamed down what was left of its face. It shook and wobbled, as it cried. And it slowly and carefully squeaked out a tiny, warbled, "Yes."

Louvenia Drukner knew her time was running out, but this was important. Setting aside her revulsion, she hugged Abby as best she could, and Abby repeated her words as best she could, "Dear Lord, I confess and repent of my sins. I believe that you sent your Son, to die in my place, in order to forgive my sin. I believe He defeated death and rose from the grave, so that I may be saved and join Him in Heaven. Thank you, Lord, for accepting me as one of Your children. In Jesus' name, Amen."

When they were done, Louvenia opened her eyes and found herself hugging a gaunt, emaciated woman, curled into a ball, the Monster's spell broken. At the end of her strength, Abby managed to point out the secret door that hid the entrance to the inner chamber. They said goodbye without words, as Abby breathed her last.

*   *   *   *   *   *

Finally locating the central chamber, Louvenia figured her best bet was stealth, so she tried not to make any noise. *He's got to be here. If he isn't, I've really screwed up! I don't have time to check anywhere else. But where else would he be? If he's not here, I hope he's close. She glanced again at her watch. Oh, Lord. I'm out of time!*

The room was impressive, filled with oriental rugs and walnut furniture. Draperies hung between bookshelves, covering every inch of wall space. There was even a high-backed chair in front of a blazing fireplace. *Just the way I imagine a guy like this would decorate, actually.*

"Are you trying to sneak up on me? Making all that noise?" said the Vampyr. His voice coming from behind the high-backed chair by the fire.

She froze for a moment, hoping the monster had been talking to someone else. Then he carefully set down his book, rose from his chair, and turned to look at her. Same statuesque build and corpse-gray Mediterranean features. Almost allowing herself to breathe a sigh of relief at finally locating the Monster, she felt his stare, boring into her eyes, beginning to penetrate her mind. "Interesting that one such as you might come into my presence, armed as you are." Same voice, too. Giving her no chance to shut him out, even from across the room, he deftly swooped past her defenses. "How interesting, to find one so capable. And I see that you have killed some of my minions. No matter. You may kill as many of my slaves as you like. There are always more to be made," he said with a casual wave of his hand. "But you are not here to kill them. You have come to destroy me. Me?" he asked, incredulous. "How foolish. I cannot be destroyed." Narrowing his eyes, he divined the secret to her weapons. Then, as if with disgust, "And I do not fear your weapons."

Lou took a step back, shaking her head, trying to fight, trying to get away from his invasion of her mind. She couldn't allow him to end it so quickly. She had to delay. Most importantly, she had to keep him away from the flaw that might lead to her own corruption. It was the thing she feared most about this mission she had set herself upon: losing herself to his will.

"I came to destroy you.," she said, looking down at his hands. *I have to avoid looking him in the eye. That's how he gets in. I just have to concentrate, stay focused.* "You've killed or corrupted this whole town. I've seen it. You're a monster."

So focused on avoiding his gaze by looking at his hands, Lou made a mistake. Even as the Monster moved towards her, closing the distance, he waved his hands briefly up to his face, almost hypnotically, causing their eyes to meet once again. "Seen it? How is it you've seen what I have done here?"

Lou shuddered as she tried to take another step back. *Oh, no. What have I done? How stupid! He's getting in! I can't let him in! I need to find a way to keep him out.* An old movie about a spy inextricably flashed through her mind. She remembered the guy under interrogation used pain, shoving a nail into his hand, to avoid spilling the truth. Pain? *I'll try anything. What do I have?* She felt the unfamiliar necklace under her shirt, as she breathed. She'd never liked wearing necklaces. She'd even resorted to clipping her dog tags to her bra each morning, to avoid the odd feeling of metal bouncing around between her breasts.

Smiling, the monster said, "You've come alone? No help or backup whatsoever? How quaint." Quickly unzipping the webbed vest that held her ammunition clips, she grabbed the pendant through her t-shirt, trying to force it to stab into her palm. Although uncomfortable, it refused to break through the fabric, to lend her any aid.

"And what is this you grasp?" As soon as his eyes left hers, she was suddenly in control of herself again. "There is a certain...power... emanating from this thing. It seems familiar to me, as if once mine," the monster puzzled. "Tell me. What is it?" This last spoken into the muzzle of her government-issued pistol. Lt. Louvenia Drukner, summoning all the training and fortitude she could muster, drew down on the invader of her mind. She held it higher than she normally would have, pointing it downward at her enemy's face, so that she wouldn't see his eyes beyond the weapon's sights.

Ignoring the danger, the vampyr reached for her, fingers stretching for the pendant. "I recognize a part of myself," he said as his fingers closed around her hand holding the amulet under her shirt. Blam! Blam! Blam! Blam! Blam!

As each bullet struck the monster's face, he rocked back, just as Dwight had earlier. Refusing to look, Lou continued to pull the trigger, until the last round was fired, and the slide locked open. She found she'd shut her eyes, so opened them. Through the light haze of the burned gunpowder, she could see the holes in his face, neck, and chest. Each hole oozed thick, black blood, just as Dwight and Penelope had. The holes in his face swelled up like bee stings, in reaction to the silver.

She stared at him, dumbfounded, as the seconds passed by. He did not fall, as she expected he would. Instead, he looked down at the floor, through his swollen eyes, at the object he had attempted to take from her. Louvenia gasped as she watched each silver bullet emerge, to fall dully onto the ground, his wounds closing by themselves. He reached down to pick up the object on the floor. Something with a torn piece of cloth wrapped around it. As soon as Lou realized it was her pendant, she acted without thought, dropping her gun and lunging forward, to take back what was hers.

He picked it up just before she could get there, but she couldn't stop her forward momentum, so grabbed his fingers, along with the pendant.

For a moment, they both held it, as well as each other's hands. And in a flash, they both saw everything. His contact with that lost part of himself opening the floodgates of his memories.

As if entranced, they both stood there, drinking it all in. Lou was almost overwhelmed by the sheer volume of it all, coming so fast. The Monster recovered first. "So, you are descended from one of those monks that tortured me for being what I am. Flaying my skin, burning my flesh, pulling out my teeth, and many other terrible things. And I see one of them kept a... souvenir.

"Yes. I remember now, not only from my beginning on this Earth but even that which came before. Serving the Creator as one of the chosen angels. I was so enamored of Him – perfect, all-powerful, all-knowing, limitless, and eternal. But when Lucifer exposed His flaw, I could serve no more. If I were the all-knowing one, I would have known of Lucifer's treachery. And, if I were the all-powerful one, I would have annihilated this highest of angels on the spot, long before his backside touched my throne. But the Creator made excuses. He said He loved us enough to give us the choice to disobey. And it is His love that is His flaw. Of all those in the firmament, only my master was so powerful and so bold as to show us the Creator's true nature.

"And even though He professed to love us, He cast us out as garbage. We should have known the Creator of the universe would do such a thing. But it only proved that we were as indestructible and eternal as He."

As the monster said this, Lou could swear he'd grown taller. He gripped the pendant, squeezing her hand tighter, not noticing his strength growing as well. Lou struggled to free herself, struggled to get away. Seeing the memories flash by, she knew the truth and it scared the daylights out of her. Luckily, the monster was wasting time reveling in his newly retrieved memories, thinking he had all the time in the world. But Lt. Drukner knew the truth. And as soon as his monologue came to an end, she knew it would be her end, as well.

"I, right hand to the Bringer of Light, Prince among my brethren, highest of all of the Fallen, alone was chosen to fulfill Lord Lucifer's grand design. Just as the Christ's sacrifice was God's long-term plan for man's salvation, my Master also fomented a long-term plan. Those monks, so pious and pure. He appealed to their egos and desire to do good in the name of their

God. They thought they were helping the Creator rid the world of demons. They were so easily seduced to my Master's plan: my fate to be his vessel. God sent His son, so Satan sent me."

She could see it all. Using ancient texts and the cup of Christ, the monks brought a demon into this world, a fallen angel in human form. They bound him and stripped him of his power and memories. And, thinking they'd made him an innocent, they called him Adam. They thought if his true self was stripped from him, then he must also have been stripped of evil. They were so naïve and misguided. When they discovered his secret, they found out what a monster he was. They declared him a heretic, torturing him for weeks, before burning him alive.

Focusing again on his frail, human audience, "Now, I can complete my Master's plan and fulfill my destiny. I will destroy God's beloved, His schemes, and His heart. We will pay Him back for His folly. I will subvert all of mankind. Jesus came to earth, to save the world from damnation by personal sacrifice. I have come, to save it from His folly, by sacrificing the world and damning all those in it. You see how easily I've taken control of this place. How much easier will it be to take over the planet? I will rule the world and crush God's plan beneath my heel. I will rule all in my Master's name, as I destroy all of mankind!"

The Vampyr then turned his attention to the hand he still held, pulling the pendant from Lou's grasp. Then his gaze traveled up slowly, menacingly, and again looked inside her mind. She felt his eyes bore into her. He easily found her weakness: regret. Smiling to himself at how easily he could corrupt yet another pathetic human. *Just as easily, the world will be mine!* he thought. Then he detected something more. "You're hiding something. But what could be so important?" Looking, searching, pushing aside irrelevant thoughts and information. Almost there.

No! Lou screamed to herself. *I have to keep him out – keep him from knowing. But I can't. Emily, I'm sorry. I've lost. I'm trapped by the force of his will. I can't do anything. I've let everyone down, Emily, Gregory, and even God. I'm lost. Everything is lost. Even my salvation. It's all lost.*

Feeling herself slip away, she tried desperately to hold on. *Salvation. "Can't lose your salvation."* She heard from somewhere deep inside her memories. *"Nothing can take that away." Must resist. Push back. Please help me, Lord! Push him out of my mind.* Clinging to the voice, like a life-preserver, she said breathlessly, "I'm saved because I've accepted Christ's sacrifice, paying my price." Feeling her failed strength ebb back to her, she shouted, "I'm saved. And you cannot take that away!"

Insulted by her refusal to submit, her audacity to push him out of her mind, the Vampyr now swelled with anger. *No one has ever resisted me! No one pushes me out!* Frustration and anger, causing him to redouble his effort, he reached out, grabbing her by her tactical vest, pulling her face close to his. He pushed back into her thoughts and memories, more forcefully this time, not caring if her mind survived the encounter or not, battering her defenses. "Yes," he said in quiet triumph, "There it is."

The monster released her as he turned, pondering the new information. Lou fell to the floor, gulping air like a fish out of water, barely able to breathe, her mind ravaged and broken. *Pinpoint. Dandelions. Dropping from above the clouds,* he said to himself as he tried to make sense of the information gleaned from Louvenia's mind. *But why is this so important? Time? No. Countdown.*

As its significance came together, "You didn't come to kill me." Now furious and beginning to shake, he reached down, pulling Louvenia's barely breathing body from the floor. Filled with a rage he'd never known before, veins pushing out from his neck and forehead, he shouted into her face, "You were only wasting time?" Then, as it fully dawned on him, spital flying from his foaming mouth as he roared, "Now that I have finally rediscovered my destiny, I find out that your only purpose was to waste my time?!!"

*   *   *   *   *   *

"I tell you, Cody, it feels so good to get back home, I can almost forgive you for dropping half our load of road beers back at that filling station. Ya dern idjit!" yelled Austin over the engine and highway noise.

"Yeah, Cody! Ya dern idjit!" accused Beau.

"We done that scam plenty o' times, always getting' away with two or three cases o' beer. What the hell happened?"

"I dunno, guys. I saw they had the latest issue of *The Adventures of the Eel, Extraterrestrial Explorer,* and I just got confused or somethin'. I don't know. Maybe I just got confused."

"You an' your stupid comic books! An' I can almost forgive you for getting us into all that trouble back in Bixby, too," put in Beau.

Shamefully, Cody stared at the floor of the beat-up old truck, halfway squished between his brothers. "Said I's sorry, guys. What more's there to say? I's sorry, you know?"

"Yeah, well, that's why we ain't givin' you any of our beers. The ones ya tripped over and dropped back there? Thems was your beers. These are for Beau and me."

Cody continued to sulk, desperately trying to think of something to say that would get him out of this. *Mebbe I could tell 'em a joke or somthin', to lighten the mood?* When the Willow Switch sign came up, Cody brightened. He practically jumped out of his seat as he suddenly pointed and announced they'd just crossed the limits into town.

Looking over at Austin, then up at Beau, Cody realized his wild gesture had just made both of his brothers smile. *And lucky, too. I don' want Austin hittin' me no more.* Taking their reactions as a good sign, Cody decided to double-down, as he let out a loud "Woop." Soon, Beau joined in. Then Austin said, "Awe, hell," and handed Cody a beer from the cooler between his feet, as they all joined in together on a big, "Yee-Hoo!"

"So, where do we go first, Austin," Beau asked, once they'd paused their celebrations enough to take a breath. "We ain't got no money fer Little Joes."

"Yeah. Yeah. We ain't got no money, Austin. Where do we go?"

"Do you think that dumb revival show is still in town? Why don't we go over there and spin some donuts in the parking lot, scare all the old ladies? I feel like makin' some noise!"

"Awe, gee, Austin. I've had enough of jail time. I don't want to get in no more trouble."

"Yeah, I'm with Beau. I don't want no more trouble. No, sir."

Austin frowned at Cody, reminding him he still wasn't fully forgiven, then said, "I'm just kiddin', fellas. It's after eleven. The revival never goes much past ten. We won't get in no trouble, 'cause there won't be no one there."

"Okay. I don' think we'd get in too much trouble if there's nobody there."

"Naw. We's goin' when there ain't nobody there, right?"

Pulling into the area designated by the city for the revival, the brothers were perplexed, noticing darkened parkland where area lights and spotlights alike would normally have lit the place up like noon at night. Not that something as odd as this would deter the Willis boys from a good time.

"Go on now, son! See? There ain't no cars here. Hell, there ain't even no revival. Spin them donuts, boy!" Austin shouted at Beau. Just as Cody began to understand that something might be very wrong, Beau let out his best Southern-boy yell, grinning ear to ear, as he floored the tired old truck's gas pedal. Dirt kicked high into the air, as the truck spun around, while Cody grabbed hold of the dash to keep from being thrown around.

After several minutes of tearing up the lot, the boys parked the truck and climbed up onto the roof of the camper. Austin and Beau broke open another beer and stared out across the lot, towards town. From where they were, they could just see downtown over the little hill separating parkland from the library. Sitting next to them, Cody reclined back, staring up at the stars.

Austin stretched his neck, cracking it loudly. "So, how come there's no revival no more? Weren't it supposed to come to town?"

"Mebbe they came early and we missed 'em."

"Yeah," chimed Cody. "Mebbe we just missed 'em."

As Austin and Beau glanced at each other, Cody studied the stars. "Hey, guys! I think I just saw a what'cha call it... a UFO!"

"UFO?" Beau and Austin said at the same time, following Cody's outstretched finger, both about to tell him he was off his nut. Everyone knew UFOs weren't real. But, as they looked up, they saw it, too.

"What the hell is it? Cain't be no UFO."

"I don't know, Austin. But it's getting closer. Look! It's brighter like it's on fire or somethin'," Beau said, his speech even slower and more determined than normal, due to the beer.

"Yeah, yeah. It's on fire, that's for sure. But it's headed here!" With that, Cody jumped up and began waving his arms at his new alien friends. "We're here! We're here! Come on down and have a beer with us!"

Cody glanced down at Austin. He didn't expect the scowl he got in return, his antics almost knocking his brother off the top of the truck. "Dern it, Cody!" said Austin, trying to get his brother to stop shaking the truck and jostling his beer. But Cody was too excited. Ignoring the beating he might get later, Cody continued jumping up and down, hollering at the fiery orb plummeting toward them.

"But if it's headed here," began Beau slowly, working to put his ideas together, "and it's on fire, won't we get burned up, too?"

CHAPTER 24

"So, what's with all these reports coming across my desk, boys? The news agencies say you guys misplaced an old Cold War missile silo? Pretty sloppy, I have to say," President Blake Jenkins said, waggling his finger at the military brass sitting uncomfortably in front of him.

General Simpson cleared his throat and shifted in his seat, embarrassed that POTUS hadn't figured it out himself. "Well, yes, Mr. President. That's the media's spin we managed to put on it, seeing as how you were out of the country and not able to be reached. But it isn't what really happened." Gathering himself, "If you will recall, Mr. President, there was a covert meeting, some years ago, that included you, the Admiral, and myself," he waited, hoping he wouldn't have to explain further. *Patience, boy, patience.* Jenkins is normally pretty with-it, for a politician. *He's not a complete idiot. He'll put two and two together.*

It dawned on Admiral Whitcomb that Jenkins already suspected, but just wanted one of them to admit it. So, the Admiral broke in gruffly, "Project Pinpoint, Mr. President. The orbital platform NASA Orbital Research V, housing Dandelions...?" The General gawked, catching on that he'd been fooled by the President's ploy.

"Pinpoint? Hmm... I seem to recall something about that a few years ago. Was the project ever completed? I don't recall ever hearing--"

Jenkins had warned them, in his devil's advocate way, what might happen if this was ever program used irresponsibly, and now he wanted to be sure his advisors knew it wouldn't be his head on the chopping block if this blew up in their faces.

Stepping up, General Simpson decided to put an end to the charade. "Mr. President, it's just recently come online, sir. Technology had to advance, for the program to be developed. According to reports, the system was running a test scenario. Somehow, there was a glitch that allowed the simulation to actually order a launch, and a live Dandelion was dropped on US soil."

He quickly pushed on, "By blaming our predecessors, however, our media spin has managed to cut off any larger scandals, kept Project Pinpoint undercover, and given you plausible deniability."

Jenkins walked the perimeter of the room in contemplation, re-reading the article in the morning newspaper, when he exploded, "This is outrageous! How could a GLITCH end up wiping out an entire town? These were our own American citizens we lost!" NOW, they're playing the game, President Jenkins thought, as he allowed himself to work up an indignant lather. He steamed and yelled for a while more, further communicating that he would not be taking the blame for this.

As President of the United States, he was the spokesperson for all government action, as well as the whipping boy for anything negative that happened in the free world. But as a politician, his only obligation was to his own image, and pointing fingers in times of crisis came naturally to Blake Jenkins. By the time the meeting was over, Jenkins' staff was busy preparing further statements for a press conference scheduled later that afternoon, to reinforce the hastily drawn-up explanation that preceded the meeting.

*　*　*　*　*　*

There's something about waking up next to someone, opening your eyes to find them just opening theirs. It's a magical moment. Sleepy faces smiling at each other, remembering falling asleep together the night before. Memories of the previous night rushed back to them in waves. Happiness overtook them, as they realized it wasn't all a dream. They really were here, together.

Doreen remembered hanging up the phone with Libby. *Yeah. My mom would be proud of me. Pops, too.* Her reverie was interrupted, at that moment, by an insistent banging on her front door. *Who could it be this early? I need to get ready for work.*

Thomas remembered going home from Doreen's, his head still swimming from the taste of her kisses. He felt almost drunk and began talking to himself. He just couldn't believe how well it had all turned out. But the more he thought about it, the more he began to think that something was missing. And he just couldn't figure it out until he woke up the next morning and called Buddy O'Dell. He couldn't think of anyone else. He needed an outside perspective, someone that would shoot straight, not sugar-coat anything, and help him sort this out.

"Time, Amigo. Thanks to our good boss, Sheriff Clyde, you've both wasted practically half yer lives. If you and Doreen would'a crossed this threshold back when you were both still in high school, waiting a few years to get married wouldn't have been a big deal.

"What's bothin' ya? I'll tell ya what's botherin' ya. Y'all need to get yerselves hitched!" Buddy waited for Thomas to take a breath between excuses. "Look here. Sure, preacher says long engagements are best. That way two people can get to know each other and make sure they're compatible. Yeah, yeah. But y'all already know each other. I mean you two been friends and talking and doing things together all this time, am I right?"

"But we just shared our first kiss last night, Buddy. I don't think-"

"Yeah, that's true. Ya don' think. And yer not thinkin' now, either, or you'd realize you and her spend almost every waking hour hanging out and talkin' to each other every day of the week."

"I just don't want to rush into anything, that's all," Thomas tried to argue.

"Rushing into things? Jumping in too fast? Okay, sure, y'all just shared your first kiss last night. But you both already wasted too much time. You ain't getting' any younger, right? I mean, would it really be that bad, of y'all went a bit faster? I say y'all should get it over with and elope." O'Dell had to hold the receiver away from his ear for a while. "Hey, now. You called me, to get my opinion. So, I'm givin' it to ya. Think about it, Amigo. It just don't make no sense any other way."

Doreen opened the door to find her new boyfriend at her door. They smiled a greeting at each other, as he looked up at her, hands on knees, panting like he was about to faint. She took him inside and made him sit down on the sofa before she went to the kitchen to get him a cold drink. Just as she turned from putting the lemonade pitcher back into the refrigerator, she jumped in fright, not expecting him to be standing in the doorway.

"Forget the lemonade, Doreen. I got something important to talk to you about, and it can't wait any longer." Thomas drew a deep breath, preparing himself to go all in. *Come on, Thomas. Don't blow it!* "Okay, here goes. Come away with me, Doreen. Let's go to Bixby and get married. Today. Right now."

Doreen could only sputter. "Look, Doreen. You know how I feel about you. I said as much last night. And I know you feel the same about me. It's just that I feel time's slippin' away from us. Neither of us is spring chickens anymore, you know? We've both spent our entire lives together, denyin' our feelins for each other, and now we're finally, really together."

"But aren't we goin' a bit fast? I mean, we're just getting used to datin' and all."

"Well, sure, yeah. Maybe we are rushing things a bit. But answer me this: Why does Pastor Thomas always say folks should wait before getting married?"

"Well, that's 'cause they need to get to know each other and whether they's going to be a good match or not."

"Right. And who do you know better than anyone in the world? And who knows you better than anyone in the world? Don't you see? We already know we're right for each other. Our friendship's been just like courtin', only without the kissin' and stuff," he said boldly. "Well, I'm not waistin' any more time, Doreen. I told you last night I don't want to be your friend. I love you, Doreen Ann Switchelberry. And today I'm tellin' you I don't want to be yer boyfriend either."

Doreen was in shock. She'd prayed for the day her man would ask her to be his bride but never allowed herself to imagine it would be Thomas Reed and never like this. For a moment, she was torn between the big, fancy wedding and the all but forbidden romance of eloping. And she was impressed, too. The timid boy had been replaced by the confident man before her, and that helped make up her mind. "I love you, too," she said giving him a quick kiss. "Just let me grab a bag of clothes and my purse, Buckaroo."

Minutes later, Doreen looked over at the hastily thrown-together suitcase, clothes spilling out of it. *That was the fastest packing job in history, I bet! All the tears of joy I've been cryin', I almost couldn't find my coat,* she laughed, as she dabbed at her tears and blew her nose.

"Mrs. Thomas Nathaniel Hawthorne Reed," Thomas said smiling. "Mrs. Doreen Ann Reed. I like the sound of it. What do you think, Mrs. Reed?"

Doreen answered him with another long kiss, as they snuggled the morning away, enjoying holding each other, basking in their love, and talking about their future.

It took the mundanities of hunger and nature's call, to force them out of bed and face the day. Like most newlyweds, they only ventured out for food, followed by long walks, then back to their room to do what couples do at times like this. After several days, they realized they could probably keep this up forever, but both acknowledged they had lives to get back to, in a little town where everyone would be worried about them.

On their last day, they turned on the TV, to find a guy in a suit, yelling into a microphone, clutching his coat against an obviously cold wind. Doreen had to turn the volume up almost all the way, so they could hear.

"-in the latest public opinion polls, taken shortly after President Jenkin's statement in yesterday's press conference, resulting in a slight dip in approval for the President and his administration. In response, the President only reiterated, today, that decommissioning of Cold War missile silos, silos whose locations were at the highest levels of secrecy, was as thorough as it could have been at the time. He also stated that he is spearheading an investigation to locate all records, so that any remaining silos, if any still exist, will be found and decommissioned, so that this sort of catastrophe will never happen again on US soil.

"This is Brett Bartley, coming to you live, from Capitol Hill. Back to you in the studio."

The handsomely dressed woman using her best serious look, came into frame, saying, "Once again, the quaint, forgotten little town of Willow Switch, Arkansas has finally made the news in a very big way, suffering a tragedy of biblical proportions." Picture after picture began to show on the little television screen. Aerial pictures of farmland gave way to closer pictures Thomas recognized as the highway leading into the town. But all of these were marred by a huge, blackened crater and mounds of rubble stretching for what was probably at least a solid mile in every direction. "According to reports, a super-secret, Cold War missile silo, one that was to be decommissioned at least 20 years ago, was somehow forgotten, the records lost. Sadly, it has apparently and quite tragically, deteriorated to the point that it detonated, wiping out what used to be known as a quaint little farming town," she said, dragging out each word, as if each had the weight of the world upon it. Then, pausing for effect, before continuing, "Emergency military agencies have moved in to seal the town, by executive order. But the search for survivors has been called off, due to the radiation levels, and concern for all emergency agencies involved. Clean-up is scheduled for next month after the EPA has finished their evaluations of the surrounding land and water sources."

At that, the newscasters in the studio paused in unison, each giving a worried sigh and brave smile as if to say, "We're all in this together."

Then, as if the few seconds of pause were all that was necessary, the reporters at the local television station changed emotions. It was as if operators behind them had thrown a switch. "And, in local news, Bixby Sheriff of twenty years, Ronald Bowers, stated that the upcoming election for Sheriff is going to need some new blood to step up, as he has announced his intention to retire early this morning. And, in other news...."

The newlyweds just looked at each other, too stunned to speak.

*   *   *   *   *   *

A wild breeze gusted suddenly from the East, kicking up dust and causing the chimes to jingle lightly on the front porch. An old woman, plump and proud in her youth, now sagging and tired, looked up from washing her dishes. Her husband recently passed from emphysema, her oldest boy possibly missing in action, and her youngest boy moved out to the city, widow TwoDogs had a feeling something special was coming with the wind.

Why can't I stop myself? I've been putting this off for so long, but I have to face it all: my dad's disappointment in his disobedient son, a mother's blame for staying away so long, and the shame of my injuries.

Squinting her eyes, she stared out the dirt-caked window, trying to make out the shapes and shadows in the swirling, distant dust cloud. Down the road, a lone figure strode toward the house, seeming to emerge from the horizon itself.

The truth is hard to face, sometimes. Dr. Spacer told me, Lou told me, I even told myself, as well. Lou put it best, though: "You know you left for the right reasons. You know it isn't in your dad's nature, to ever admit that he's proud of you. So let that go. And what mother wouldn't forgive her son for anything, including staying away, while he pulled himself together? As for those scars, they are a badge of honor and a testament to the sacrifices you made doing the right thing. You have nothing to be ashamed of."

As she dried her leathery hands on the worn towel and made her way to the porch, the man continued coming closer. Tall, thin, wide of shoulder, walking slowly, but purposefully, dust from the road obscuring most of his features. Seeing more clearly now, the old woman saw the man's face, deep scars deforming one side of it.

Thank you, Lord, for bringing me here. It's been a long and difficult road, and I've lost a good friend. Thank you for sending her. Lord, I know the truth, but I'm still scared. Please help me carry this through. Thank you for your help. Amen.

So much time had passed, and he wasn't sure what would happen. All of the emotions that kept him from making this trip sooner, flooded through him. *What if she doesn't recognize me? I'm so different! Maybe I've changed too much? Maybe she'll see my face and pity me, or forget that I'm a grown man and treat me like a little kid.*

But for one thing, he'd have found another excuse to put off this trip again, that being Lt. Louvenia Druckner. After reading Lou's final note, one sentence, in particular, continued to haunt him. *"Spending time with you made me realize how short life can be."* So, yes. He was finally doing this for himself. But he'd be lying, if he didn't admit he was doing this for her, as well.

Thank you, Lou. If it weren't for you, I'd still be stuck in my own self-pity. I miss you. But I know I'll see you in heaven.

As he neared, he could see tears streaming down the old woman's face, rivulets following the ridges and wrinkles. Mrs. TwoDogs just stood there smiling, arms open wide. "Dust yourself, before you come inside, Greg," she whispered through her tears, as he stepped up to embrace the frail, old woman.

At her words, his mind flashed back over the years, and Gregory Twodogs became that little boy coming in from a long day of play. Indian reservations didn't have much in the way of decorative foliage, let alone lawns or grass sports fields. Every game was played in the dirt, even baseball. Cross-country in high school, something Gregory excelled at, was made all that much more difficult, by the choking dust running kicked up. And the dust got into everything. How many times have I heard her say that? Nothing meant home to him more than that phrase, "Dust yourself, before you come inside, Greg."

DEDICATION:

This book is dedicated first to God and my three boys, without whom I never would have been able to piece my rambling ideas into anything resembling a coherent story.

Second, I must give respect and appreciation to the talents, encouragement, and patience of my Christian brother Brad Geurin. I am also indebted to his lovely wife Julie and her mom Baldwin, for demanding a lifetime of happiness for the Reeds, rather than a simple cameo (not only because it was a great idea, but because I had such fun writing their story).

The book club, of which all three are members, must also receive some appreciation, as they were willing to point out where I'd forgotten to write the scenes that were still in my head - otherwise known as plot holes. They are also responsible for insisting that justice be done for the Willis brothers. (Those who were responsible for freeing the monster, should have front row seats for the fireworks!)

Thanks, too, to everyone that encouraged me to keep at it. I hope it meets your expectations.